Lock Down Publications and Ca$h
Presents

THA TAKEOVER 2

FROM THE START

Written By
KEITH CHANDLER

First Edition 2025

Printed in the United States of America

This is a work of fiction. Names, characters, places, and incidents either are products of the author's imagination or are used fictitiously. Any similarity to actual events or locales or persons, living or dead, is entirely coincidental.

Lock Down Publications
P.O. Box 944
Stockbridge, GA 30281
www.lockdownpublications.com

Like our page on Facebook: Lock Down Publications
www.facebook.com/lockdownpublications.ldp

Stay Connected with Us!

Text **LOCKDOWN** to 22828 to stay up-to-date with new releases, sneak peaks, contests and more…

Like our page on Facebook:
Lock Down Publications

Join Lock Down Publications/The New Era Reading Group

Visit our website:
www.lockdownpublications.com

Follow us on Instagram:
Lock Down Publications

Email Us: We want to hear from you!

Acknowledgements

First, I want to give all my praise to God. It's because of you that I've come this far. Next, I would like to give a big thanks to my cousin James Bryant, aka Baby J, for helping me write this book and pushing me to get up and finish it when we were in the cell together.

I would also like to thank the following list of people: my mother, my pops, all my sisters, my brothers, my three daughters, my two aunties, my uncle, Rachel, Lindsey, cousin Branden (Post Road), Marcus (Due), Scrill (South Bend), Tommy Gunz (Kenwood), Buddha (4-Block), my cousin Jackie, and her husband. And to my bro Dustin Perkins, aka Nasty, love, bro.

In my next book, I would like to give my kids half. The other half, I would like to get together with the mayor of Indianapolis so that I can split my half to help kids in the Urban community.

If you have any suggestions, you can write to me:

Keith Chandler #149902
P.O. Box 1111
Carlisle, IN 47838

Prologue

Inside the gray brick and stained white walls of the federal courthouse, located in downtown Indianapolis, Murrell "Uno" Brandon and Rodney "LR" Brew were on trial for their lives. Uno and LR sat calmly beside their female lawyers, Desiree Star and Amaya Star. Uno and LR were seated calmly and relaxed in their black Gucci suits with black gators, waiting for the jury to come back.

The WSF organization, supposedly led by Uno and LR, was responsible for the murders of just about anyone who stepped in their path to the top. The government wanted the two put away for the rest of their lives, and they didn't want anything or anyone to get in the way of that. The two were considered the biggest things to come out of Indianapolis in the last fifteen years. The organization was feared by many.

Uno and LR had been charged with racketeering and conspiracy to purchase and distribute more than a thousand kilograms. For years, the authorities tried to link them to the hundreds of bodies that appeared and disappeared along the path of violence. The type of vicious Uno and LR released on the streets quickly earned them their seat at the top of the FBI's most-wanted list. As far as the DEA and the ATF were concerned, there wasn't anybody more dangerous walking the streets of Indianapolis.

Uno glanced around the courtroom at all the people crowded inside. The faces of family members, friends, enemies, victims, officers, reporters, and ghosts from the past sat and waited to see the outcome of the biggest trial Indianapolis had seen.

Working her way up from the bottom of her class to become the best-known criminal defense lawyer in the country, Desiree stood five feet and two inches tall, but when she stood in the courtroom, it was as if she were a giant. She gave respect and demanded it in return, and she had established a great deal of rapport among her colleagues. She knew the right moment to inflect her voice. It was the biggest case of her career, and she knew the stakes were high, but no matter what, she made sure to bring her A-game.

It had been a long four months of exhibits, photographs, witnesses, objections, and explanations. Every day seemed longer than the one before. It was the final day, and the verdict would be read.

Judge Melvin B. Webster leaned back in his seat, giving his back a rest for the first time that day. Taking a deep breath, Mr. Webster closed his eyes momentarily, wondering when he'd taken the turn to arrive at that point in his life. Mexican by birth, born to immigrant parents who made their first home as a family in the United States in California, he had seen so much during his sixty-five years on earth. His face was clean with a thin mustache and a bald head.

Serving as a federal judge for nearly twenty years, he had seen things change. He had power and intelligence about himself. From the smallest to the biggest, criminals couldn't escape his gravity. The case had a great deal of attention on it from the press, as well as behind closed doors, where a lot of powerful people silently had their hands involved. The case was about much more than Murrell "Uno" Brandon and Rodney "LR" Brew.

Judge Webster looked around the courtroom at the many faces. The courtroom fell silent before Judge Webstar could get his hands on his gravel. It was like the judge and the courtroom had an understanding.

"Mr. Foreman, did the jury reach a final verdict?" Judge Webster asked, clearing his throat.

"Yes, we have, your honor," the foreman said as he stood.

The bailiff then walked over and was handed a folded piece of paper. Everyone's eyes in the courtroom followed the paper from the jury box to the judge's hand.

The judge leaned down to grab the paper from the bailiff. He glanced at the paper and folded it back up. "Mr. Brandon and Mr. Brew, will you please stand for the reading of your verdict?" Judge Webster asked, looking at Desiree and Amaya.

Chapter 1

The Beginning
Indianapolis, Indiana
Fifteen years earlier...

"Chow time, five minutes! Chow time, five minutes!" the CO yelled over the intercom in the dorm.

Getting off his bunk, Uno grabbed his morning hygiene and headed to get ready.

"You walking over there with me, cuz?" Uno asked.

"What? Hell naw! You know I'm not fucking with that trash shit, and I don't understand why you keep going to chow when we got all this food in this room," Baby J replied, flipping through some new pictures Uno received the night before from Big Dawg or Ant. He was looking at all the new fashion.

Enthusiasm was the reason Baby J paced the room all night. After spending his last two birthdays in the state boy school, that day, the state would release Baby J before his fifteenth birthday. The state was only letting people go home who had a few months left on their sentences.

A week before, Baby J was called out to his counselor's office and informed that the state wanted him released. Ever since that day, Baby J's mind had been in overdrive, thinking about everything possible.

Imagining his mom's and Grannie's cooking, Baby J licked his lips.

Uno opened his box to put his hygiene back and check his fade in the mirror. Late the night before, he had Baby J fade him up so the waves in his hair did a 360 around his head.

"Damn, cuz! At least walk with a nigga!" Uno yelled from the mirror.

"Aight, nigga, you got that!" Baby J replied, getting off his bunk.

Uno smiled as he watched Baby J walk up to him.

"Give big cuz some love," Baby J said with his arms open.

Honestly, both were emotional and hurt. They were going to miss each other like hell. After sharing the same room for the last two years, the two had grown closer than they were on the streets, and they shared a lot of the same interests. Some nights, they would stay up, talking about some of the trouble they used to be in, out in the world.

Uno and Baby J were second cousins. Baby J, his mother, and his brother, Bird, used to stay with Uno's mother. It was known throughout the boy school that if you fucked with one, you had to deal with both, and dudes already knew what that meant—trouble. Even though both of them knew how to throw their hands, Baby J was more laid back, whereas Uno constantly stayed putting his hands on someone. It got so bad that Baby J already knew when he stepped out those gates, Uno was going to turn the heat up on niggas. At five-three, toting around 175 pounds, Uno was good-looking and brown-skinned with a fade that Baby J cut once a week. Baby J toted around 190 pounds, standing at five-six, dark skinned, with long braids.

Baby J gathered all his belongings while Uno finished doing him. He smiled to himself while taking down the rest of his pictures. He had his mind set—if his family wasn't on the same page as him, then they could kick rocks, and that went for anyone.

"What time cuz 'posed to be here?" Uno asked.

"I think around nine in the morning," Baby J replied.

"So, cuz, are you goin' to holla at ol' girl for me?" Uno inquired, looking at Baby J move around the room.

Baby J smiled. "I'ma swing past there after I walk with you," he said, grabbing Uno around the shoulders as they walked and talked.

Creased down from head to toe in state-issues, both swaggered to the chow hall like they were dressed to go on a visit. Walking up the walkway, both exchanged farewell daps with all the dudes they knew or respected.

When they stepped inside the chow hall, Uno grabbed his food, while Baby J opted for an apple juice. Sitting down in their usual spots in the back, Baby J briefed Uno on any and everything he needed to know about the dealings he had done. For the past year and a half, they had the boy school cracking with weed and tobacco.

"Listen. That nigga C-murder from my way owes me $150, Yammy owes three hundred dollars, Rob and Lil' Jay trying to grab a few grams of loud, and Anthony Larossa and Cody from out south get a QP and a few cups of tobacco. Them two already paid last night. It's a little over a pound of weed and two pounds of tobacco in the spot, and that should hold you up 'til my brother or yours holla at ol' girl out there," Baby J said, looking around the chow hall.

Uno just smiled as he listened to Baby J. It was always about business with him. "Damn, I'ma miss you, cuz," Uno said.

"Nigga, you touch down real soon. Just lay back and stack some money up. I'ma have shit popping by the time you come home. Plus, you know I only have two months of papers. Shit about to be popping. My fifteenth birthday is coming up, so I'm goin' to do it big," Baby J said with a smirk on his face.

After they departed from the chow hall, Uno headed to bust a few moves before he had to go into school for his test, while Baby J swaggered to his counselor, Ms. Long's, office to say goodbye.

Knock, knock, knock. Baby J pushed open the door. Ms. Long's face lit up like a Christmas tree when she saw Baby J's face as he stood there, accosting Ms. Long's body.

She remembered a year and a half before, when Baby J and Uno walked into her office, looking all fresh. Flashbacks of when she, Bird, and Ant went to school together played in her mind like a movie. Kids in school picked on her, but Bird and Ant were the only ones to come to her aid, and from there on, they built a friendship. Tears threatened to fall from her eyes as she remembered how the two were always there to comfort her when they saw her crying in the hallways.

"I need you to get at cuz," Baby J said.

"Anything for y'all. Just let me know, and it's done," she said, shaking her head at how much Baby J looked like his cousin Ant.

"Look. The fam is goin' to pull up on you a few times for Uno. Please make sure he get his shit," Baby J said. "I know you told Ant and Bird when me or Uno got released, you would stop bringing in the stuff, but you know how family is to us! So really, neither of us can just stop the show. Feel me?" Baby J replied.

"Okay, I'm goin' to hit the family on my lunch break. You just make sure you don't come back, and I will see," Ms. Long said, pushing Baby J out of her office.

***

"Mr. Williams, report to R and R!" Baby J heard over the intercom as he headed back to the unit to grab up his stuff.

"Damn, nigga, you act like you don't wanna go to the crib, taking all day and shit!" Uno said, walking into the room.

Baby J smiled. "Cuz, if I didn't take my time, you would be hit."

"So I'm good then?" Uno asked.

"Fo' sho!" Baby J replied. After giving out dap, Baby J looked around the dorm and yelled, "See y'all on the other side!" Then he and Uno took off toward R and R.

During the walk, Baby J explained to Uno that he had to come up with a drop for Ms. Long. Baby J wore a smile on his face, making him look like the Kool-Aid Man. So many dudes came out to see him off. Even a lot of the women officers were out there, waving. By the time they hit R and R, they got a little emotional.

"Love, cuz," Baby J said, hugging Uno. "I'll see you soon."

Ten minutes later, Baby J was being escorted to the front gate with all his teeth showing. It felt so good to be dressed in something other than the boy school issues.

"Look at my baby!" was the first thing he heard when the gates opened. Baby J's mom was running toward him with her arms open and tears coming down her face. His brother walked up to get his love as well. After a few minutes, they loaded back into Bird's F-250 while Baby J looked at the boy school's walls, thinking that would never be him again.

"Let's get up outta here!" Baby J said.

Chapter 2

Fast forward two months…

Big Dawg's Mercedes-Benz cruised through the streets as Uno twisted and turned in his seat, trying to see who was who. He was amazed at how Indianapolis looked like a whole new city. Stores and new buildings were everywhere.

'You can tell I been gone for two and a half years,' he thought as they passed a block that looked like a car show. Uno couldn't believe all the cars they passed were foreign and sitting on rims. When he looked harder, he noticed a few nobodies, and some females were riding in their cute little cars.

'Damn, it's niggas my age out riding. I'm about to be fourteen. I have to step my game up. Fuck shining off my brothers,' Uno thought to himself, shaking his head, smiling, and rubbing his hands together.

Being locked up did something to Uno, so he took the last two months to better himself and the situation for those around him. Taking what he knew, was taught, and saw, he and Baby J took over the boy school, which he was going to do to the streets.

When Big Dawg whipped his Mercedes down his mother's block, the first thing he saw was a banner that read, 'Welcome Home.' All Uno could do was smile and shake his head. His mom's house looked really good on the outside, and he remembered her telling him she did a little something.

"Damn!" Uno said, staring at all his family standing in front of the house. As soon as he stepped out of the car, the family started cheering. Giving out love and daps, Uno made his way through. Uno was in a rush to see one person, his best friend.

She was one of the few people who held him down with pictures, letters, money, and phone calls. That made him love her even more. Even though they were both single, and he knew he would pursue a relationship, he wanted to step his game up because she'd dated a few older guys, and he wanted her to look at him like the boss he was.

Uno shook his head as he saw Punkin standing there, looking good. She looked better than the last time he saw her. Punkin's mom drove her up to see him one time, but after that, it flooded through the boy school that Uno had the girl from 'Everybody Hates Chris' in the visiting room.

The whole time Uno was walking toward her, she was doing her own inspection of Uno. She smiled at how fine Uno had gotten. It had been over a year since they last saw each other. His arms and chest had gotten bigger, and his hair was wavier. Making her way down his body, her eyes went to his dick print. She licked her lips as she made her way back up his body.

"Look at yourself, lookin' all edible," Punkin said as the two hugged and kissed.

As everybody made it into the house, Punkin handed him his chain and ring that Big Dawg and Ant gave her to hold for him.

Putting the chain on and sliding the ring on his finger, he kissed it.

A few hours later, the whole block was in full swing. The men all drank, played cards, and talked about the streets. The kids played amongst themselves, while the women cooked and did their own thing. Uno and Punkin sat in a chair off in a corner, talking amongst themselves. Uno looked up and smiled at everything that was going on.

"Let me holla at you for a hot second," Big Dawg told Uno.

"I'll be back, bae," Uno said, following Big Dawg to the porch where Ant, Bird, and Slow stood, sipping on beers.

Everyone had big Kool-Aid smiles on their faces when they stepped to the porch.

"Look at you, bro!" Big Dawg opened his arms, and the two hugged.

"Man, this shit crazy around here, bro. Everything changed," Uno reasoned as they released each other.

"Where my cuz, Bird?" Uno asked Baby J's brother.

"That lil' nigga out, posted, turning the heat up on them young niggas," Bird said.

"Let him know I'm home," Uno replied.

"Here," Big Dawg said, handing Uno a stack of money. "That's five grand. Put it up," he said.

"Thanks, bro. I really appreciate y'all keeping me and Baby J books laced and handling that other thing for us," Uno said to all.

"So, what's your plan?" Big Dawg asked, staring Uno in the eyes to see if he was going to lie to him about what he was going to do.

"Get a feel of this shit and try to get me some pussy from Punkin," Uno said with a smile on his face, thinking about how he'd be her first.

Everybody on the porch shook their heads.

"Have a seat," Ant said, pushing out a chair for him to sit in.

"Okay, these streets ain't sweet. You have to take the good with the bad, and you have to be a cold muthafucka. It's a difference in walkin' this life and only knowing about the life! Feel me?" Big Dawg said.

"Hell naw. If everything was perfect, you would never learn, and you would never grow," Bird said, puffing on a blunt.

"Lil' bro, I want you to go to school and say fuck all the other shit, but I know your lil' bad ass is goin' to do what you want to do, so I'm goin' to drop this on you. Always be your own leader. If you pull that pistol, use it, and most importantly, we not impressed about a nigga killing someone; we impressed by the nigga that's taking care of his family. Build your own shit," Ant said.

"If you build your own circle, you will go to the top. I see a lion in you, and I know you hungry, so eat and respect. Blessed is he who expects nothing, for he shall never be disappointed," Slow said.

Every last one of them took turns dropping jewels on Uno. Big Dawg grabbed Uno by the shoulders and gave him some last-minute jewels.

"Everybody out for self and tryna outdo the next person. These little niggas don't want to put sweat, blood, and tears in this shit. The only thing they want is a handout. Some of these little niggas are the same ones that you grew up with. Whoever have the dope and money, no matter if they rats or say everybody want to ride they dicks," Big Dawg said. "Make sure you plan for your life. Remember, life is a gamble, but you have a better chance than these other niggas out here." Big Dawg pointed at his brain. "Your mind can take you anywhere you wanna go. The more you train your mind, the more it grows because it's a miracle! I know you have a lot goin' on up there," Big Dawg said, pointing to Uno's head. "But one thing for sure is if you do go out in them streets, causing hell, nothing better not land on my momma's doorstep, because then you goin' to have to see us."

***

The next morning, around nine a.m., Uno got dressed and grabbed his keys to the old scooter his mom had put up for him when he got sent to boy school. Headed out the door to the mall, he wanted to be one of the few people there when the doors opened. Walking toward his scooter on the side of the house, he spotted an all-white Jag slowly coming down the block.

'Who the hell is this, riding like this?' he thought to himself as he started backing up toward the house. Uno stood back on the porch with a mug on his face. The driver stopped and backed up in front of the house, let down the window, and showed his face.

"Uno, is that you? I heard you came home yesterday."

Trying to make out the voice, Uno slowly moved toward the car to put a face with the voice. "It's me, nigga! Man-Man!"

Uno's eyes almost popped out of his face. When Uno got sent to boy school, Man-Man was a dirty, scared dude. Man-Man was currently riding a Jag, draped in ice, golds in his mouth, and sporting the newest threads, and he was only a year older than Uno. Uno smiled on the inside because no matter what Man-Man had going on, he would always be that scared dude he knew growing up. He also didn't like Man-Man because he used to talk to Punkin, and when she didn't give up the pussy, he kicked her to the curb.

"Damn, nigga! You done got big!" Man-Man said, stepping out of the car and giving Uno fake love.

Uno's eyes kept wandering over Man-Man's expensive jewelry, and Man-Man saw it, so he kept twisting his ring.

'This bitch out here doing it for real,' Uno thought.

"Check, dog. I know how it is when you just coming home, so here's a little something to get you by," Man-Man said, handing him twenty hundred-dollar bills. Next, Man-Man wrote down his number. "I know you goin' to chill for a while, but hit me up if you need a job, and by the looks of that old ass scooter, I know you goin' to be calling. I remember when you pulled that old thing out the hood— thought you were the shit," he added before hopping back in the car and honking his horn.

Uno stood there in astonishment with Man-Man's number in his hand. *"Hit me if you need a job?"* he said to himself, then crumbled the paper and tossed it in the street.

The mall was packed early, but then again, he heard the new Jordans were coming out, plus it was a Friday. For the next few hours, Uno balled his heart out. It felt so good to be home. As he swagged from store to store, he saw people he hadn't seen in years. Females were throwing their numbers at him, and he was loving it.

After chomping down his food, he headed over to Hat World to grab himself a few hats. While he searched the wall for something he liked, he smiled when he spotted his nigga Nasty's cousin Ashley looking at female hats on the other side of the store. Looking at Ashley's fat ass, Uno couldn't do anything but shake his head. He'd been trying to fuck Ashley since he'd met her, but she always blew him off, saying he was too young.

"Ashley, what's good?" Uno asked with a smirk.

"Oh, shit," Ashley said, lost for words at how fine Uno had gotten.

"You know your cousin only have a few weeks left up top," he told her.

Ashley hadn't heard anything he said; she was too busy feeling him out. Taking a piece of paper and a pen, she wrote down her number and address for him.

"Nigga, you know what time it is with me. Hit me up when you get yourself together," Ashley said, strutting off with extra in her walk.

By the time Uno arrived at his scooter, he was tired. He was about to throw his bag inside the department under the seat when a black Cadillac truck pulled up, and someone yelled his name.

"Uno! Long time, no see!" the driver said, hopping out.

"Baby J, what's good, big cuz?" Uno asked, smiling.

"It's me in the flesh!" Baby J replied, showing a mouth full of vvs at the top and the bottom.

"Look at you, all iced out and shit." Uno laughed. Baby J came home running. For the last few months, he'd been turning up the heat on the niggas out post, pushing weed.

Uno noticed Baby J's eyes were slanted. "You out here doin' yo' thang, I see," Uno commented.

"You know my name stamped with the best out here!" Baby J bragged. "Hop in and fuck wit' me for a little while."

After locking the scooter back up, Uno hopped in with Baby J, and they cruised around the city, passing blunts back and forth while Baby J stopped to make stings along the way.

"This some good shit! What you hittin' for?" Uno asked.

"You little cuz, so you can get it the same price I got it for," Baby J said.

***

Ashley opened the front door, wearing nothing but a pair of red pumps. Her perfume slapped him in the face as he stood with his mouth open as she stepped to the side. Once Uno was inside her parents' house, she didn't waste any time getting down to business.

Uno was fresh out, and she wanted the dick before he started passing it out. She walked Uno to the love seat and pushed him into it. Bending over in front of him, she started fingering her pussy in front of his face. Uno's dick grew the more she played and moaned. After cumming all over her fingers, she put them in her mouth and sucked all her cum off.

No one would have known Ashley had birthed two kids, because her genetics looked like she worked out or ran track, and she had a few stretch marks. Besides that, her body was tight. Ashley still looked the same as he remembered. The only thing was that she got taller and thicker, and her hair was longer.

"Is this what you been wanting?" Ashley asked Uno as she stood in front of him.

Uno's dick print said all she needed to know. He'd been wanting to fuck Ashley for so long. He couldn't hold it back any longer. Standing up, Uno took control of things, undressing down to his boxers and shoes. It was Ashley's turn to see what she'd been missing out on.

'Damn,' she thought to herself.

"Bend over," Uno said, stroking his penis. For the next ten minutes, Uno pounced on her from the back, making her cum twice.

"Boy, if I knew the dick was this good, I would have been letting you hit," Ashley said, standing up and leading Uno to her bedroom for round two.

Chapter 3

That day marked a full month since Uno had his newfound freedom. He was so focused on trying to learn who was who that he didn't notice four weeks had passed by. In the midst of things, he made sure to check in on Ms. Long a few times. He even talked to Nasty on his office phone, trying to pass the time because all Nasty had to do was hit him on the burnout phone he had. Nasty had a week left before he would be home.

Every day, Uno would get dressed and head over to Nasty's big brother Gee's trap spot and fuck with him, but in between time, he watched and listened to everything moving in and out of Gee's spot. Gee was moving pounds after pounds.

"Damn, Uno! When you get out, nigga?" Lil' Jay, Ashley's lil' brother, asked when he walked into the trap and noticed Uno sitting at the table.

"Nigga, look at you! You look good. Let's step out and burn this," Lil' Jay suggested, holding up a fat blunt.

Uno, Gee, and Lil' Jay passed the blunt back and forth for the next few minutes while chopping it up about the old times when Uno, Lil' Jay, and Nasty used to beat dudes their ages and older. When the blunt was over, Lil' Jay and Uno exchanged numbers, and Lil' Jay hopped in an Audi A8 and sped off.

"Damn, this bitch is popping!" Uno said to Gee as he went into the trap.

'*Years ago, my brothers had it popping like this with the dope. Now it's weed,*' he thought as his phone rang.

"Hello?" he picked up.

"Hey, baby. I miss you so much," Punkin said.

Hearing Punkin's voice on the other line put a smile on his face. "Aye, I miss you too, baby," Uno replied

"I didn't want anything but to hear your voice, so I'm goin' to let you get back to what you was doing," Punkin said before hanging up.

Uno stood on the porch, cautiously surveying the block, looking for anything suspicious, before heading back into the trap. Gee was moving around the tap, stacking up pounds while listening to a Young Dro mixtape, when Uno entered. The whole table was stacked with money with different colored bands on them.

"Damn, all them pounds about to be sold?" Uno asked as he took a seat next to Gee.

"Nigga, you know if your brothers find out you been in here, they goin' to kick your ass," Gee said. "Shit is jumping today!" Gee looked over and caught Uno staring off into Lala Land.

"Damn, lil' bro! I know that look!" he said, getting up. "It's about dat time. When the lion is hungry, it eats, and I know you one, so get your own! Sack nothing but the best and get some of this money."

As soon as Uno left, he called his cousin Baby J and placed an order for a few pounds. Once they finished going over numbers, they agreed to meet the next morning.

Chapter 4

Within a few days, Uno had the whole ten pounds he had copped off his cousin gone and had made over twenty-four thousand dollars after selling each ounce for six hundred dollars apiece. Knowing how Gee's trap moved, he knew it was going to be easy money, but weed wasn't profitable if it was smoked. Plus, it didn't give the rush of dope when moving blocks.

He saw Gee in the kitchen a lot, whipping dope up, so he was going to see how the dope game was, but still move weed. After grabbing Gee's five thousand dollars, Uno called Baby J to place another order.

Since Uno hadn't been spending that much time with Punkin, he decided he would surprise her. Heading over to Punkin's job at her grandparents' restaurant, he stopped and grabbed a bear, some chocolate, and a few single roses. Punkin was with a customer when he walked through the door. When she turned around, she saw Uno standing in the waiting area, holding a big, white bear, the chocolate, and the roses. She made eye contact with him and smiled as her heart melted.

Punkin would always be his heart. Not only did she hold him down during his bid, but since he'd been home, she'd been spending her little checks, buying him clothes, getting her aunt Sherry to rent cars for him, amongst other things. Uno put every dime she spent to the side. Since Punkin wanted to go to college for hair, he would make that happen for her. He just hated that she had to work at the restaurant because Man-Man's mom owned the building next to it.

"Aww, this is so sweet!" she said while smelling the roses. "Baby," she said, looking at him suspiciously.

"Just go get ready," he said, walking back out the door.

When she walked out, Uno had the car door open for her, which made her wink at him.

"Bae, what are you up to?" she asked him when he got into the car.

"Why I gotta be up to something?" Uno smirked as he pulled off. "Naw, that's just for being beautiful, girl," Uno charmed.

"Boy, boo. You're crazy as hell," she responded, blushing.

For a few minutes, they drove while listening to Lil' Chat until they pulled up in front of Punkin's mom's house.

"Listen, baby. Go throw on something real nice, and pack a bag. You spending some time wit' me. I be back soon."

"Okay, let me get out of here," Punkin said, cheesing as she hopped out and rushed up to the house.

When he arrived back at his mom's crib, he got down to business, getting himself together for the night.

Meanwhile, Punkin was hopping out of the shower, applying lotion over her body before spraying Uno's favorite perfume in the air. Next, she threw on a sexy Calvin Klein dress she got from her auntie, putting on a pair of Sarah Flint heels to finish off her look.

By the time Punkin was walking down the stairs, Uno was pulling up in front of the house. Quickly putting lip gloss on her luscious lips, she grabbed her belongings and headed out the door.

"Damn," Uno said, observing how sexy Punkin looked with her hair pinned up to show off her pretty face. He shook his head at the thought of being home a month and a half and only hitting it twice, but it was more than sex with him. He saw a real future with her.

"You looking good and smell even better," Uno complimented as he kissed her. Uno pulled off, heading to their destination. Not long after pulling off, they were pulling up to the West Inn hotel. After valet parking, the two headed inside to check in. Uno had an enchanting night planned.

"Mr. and Mrs. Brandon," Uno told the desk clerk with a big smile. "Also, I would like to have a platter of garlic grilled shrimp sent to my room, please," Uno said, handing the desk clerk a wad of cash. You can keep the change," he said, walking off.

Since the busboy took all their bags to the room, Uno decided to kill time and take Punkin on a little walk downtown. The night was beautiful, with the stars shining brightly. Twenty minutes later, the two laughed and giggled as they walked into their room. Their bags sat by the door, and the table was set for two with their food sitting in front of two candles.

"Baby, this is so sweet," Punkin said, crying.

"Stop crying, baby, and have a seat," Uno said, pulling out her chair so they could eat and talk.

As they enjoyed each other, they romantically fed one another, not realizing hours had passed by.

Getting up, Punkin immediately stripped out of her dress and walked over to the radio to put on her slow mix. Uno walked over to the bed and lay back like a fat mac. Uno smiled as Punkin, wearing nothing, approached the bed, and his dick got hard. Punkin looked at him, smiled, and then eased onto the bed. Bending down, she kissed his lips.

"Baby, tonight is your night. I want you to sit back," Uno said.

"Not happening," Punkin said, feeling the effects of the wine cooler she'd drunk. Getting on all fours, she looked at him and said, "I want you to tear this pussy up tonight."

Getting up, Uno walked behind her and slapped her ass cheeks, watching the little ass she had jiggle. She arched her back, and Uno grunted.

"Damn. Big, juicy pussy. I'ma tear this shit up. You know I'ma go hard on you tonight, don't you?" Uno asked, smiling. "Spread your legs, baby," Uno demanded, looking at her little cheeks and pussy from the back.

"Suck this pussy, muthafucka," she said, glancing at him from over her shoulder.

Bending down, he flicked his tongue over her asshole, then he kissed it before dipping it in.

"Baby, I love the way you're making love to this ass." She moaned loudly. She eyed him over her shoulder, licking her lips.

His hard, chiseled body was positioned behind her with sweat. His scrumptiously thick, seven-inch dick stabbed at the center of her pussy teasingly. He pulled open her ass again, then buried his face in it.

"Yeah, baby! Eat it up, nigga. Lick this sweet hole. Hmhmm, make love to it with that thick, wet tongue."

Two hard smacks stung her ass, causing her pussy to clench.

"Oh, yes, baby. I need to feel you inside me."

Uno stroked his dick with his hand. She coaxed him into putting a finger in her asshole. Jabbing his middle finger inside, he slowly fingerfucked her ass, getting it ready for a deep fucking.

Reaching under herself, Punkin played with her clit, getting herself wetter.

"You ready for this dick?"

"I stay ready, nigga," she said, jiggling her ass for him.

He stabbed his dick deep inside her ass.

"Hmm, yes, that's it. Fuck this ass, nigga. Oh, yes, baby. Don't be scared to beat it up".

He started fucking her faster, pounding her mercilessly, reaching his hand under her and toying with her clit. She moaned, and he groaned as he thrust into her again and again.

"Damn, ma. Ah, shit. God dammit. Mutherfuck. This ass is good!" He groaned.

"Beat it up then, nigga! Yeah, you got all that dick in this ass, baby. What's my name, nigga?" she asked.

He grunted as her hole clenched around his shaft. "Punkin, ma. Ah, fuck. Damn." His body jerked as he tightly grabbed her waist. "Mm. Ah. Mph."

"Give me that nut, nigga. Got this ass wide open. Cum all up in this ass, baby. I'm jabbing two fingers upward into my pussy, stroking my G-spot. There ya go, nigga. Fuck this ass. Oh, yes! I'm cumming!" She felt his spasm shoot through her as he pumped harder inside her. A few minutes later, he pulled out and coated her ass and back.

***

The next morning, Uno dropped Punkin off at home and then headed out to the mall to meet Baby J. He arrived at the mall and parked in the back so he could see the whole parking lot. He placed his gun on his hip, threw the backpack in the trunk, and headed inside, where he grabbed a bite to eat from a place called Dionne's Soul Food that sat in the food court, waiting for Baby J's call.

Halfway through his meal, he got the call. Baby J explained he was waiting for his connect to come through, but he knew where he could get the same stuff at the same price. After Baby J gave him a new address, he got up to throw away his trash and head out.

As Baby J was pulling up to the address, Uno pulled behind him and shut the engine off. The front door swung open, and they were instructed to go inside. When they walked into the house, they immediately began scanning their surroundings to ensure they were alone. Keeping his back to the wall and gun in hand, Uno was ready to get down to business.

"I will be out there in a hot second," a voice said from the back.

Uno knew his cousin wouldn't set him up, but he didn't know who the dude was, and he didn't trust him. Uno removed the backpack and set it on the floor in front of him. Dude was already prepared. Uno's pounds were on the kitchen table, stacked up. There was a sofa off in the corner. *'I know this muthafucka ain't getting shit through the furniture company,'* Uno thought.

"You got the money?" the voice asked as the person walked into the room.

Uno picked up the backpack, threw it to him, then walked up and grabbed one of the pounds off the table to inspect it.

"Is this the same shit my cuz got?" Uno asked, sniffing the buds. "What's ya name? You look like someone I know."

"First, yes, it's the same as your cuz, and second, my name is Flow. I have family from around ya way."

Uno looked at Baby J, who scanned the house because something didn't feel right.

"Yo, Flow, let me use ya restroom," Uno said.

"Down the hall. It's the first door on the left."

Uno headed down the hallway, snooping. He didn't have to use the restroom. He just wanted to see what else was in the house. Looking into one of the rooms, he saw more boxes. Uno peeked back down the hall, and when he saw Baby J talking to him, he slipped into that room. Looking inside one of the boxes, he saw club pictures of him with females, some of him, Man-Man, and other niggas. Uno gritted his teeth and nodded his head. Grabbing the duct tape off Flow's dresser, he charged into the living room.

"Did you find it?" Flow asked as he continued counting the last stack of money.

When Flow didn't get a response, he looked up only to see the barrel of Uno's Glock pointed at his face and Baby J's vvs shining. "Bro, what's happening?" Flow stuttered with sweat beads dripping down his face.

"Man, fuck all this talking! Get up!" Uno ordered.

Flow quickly jumped to his feet.

"Now, I want ya to listen. You have two choices. We can do this the hard way or the easy way. The choice is up to you. Now, I'ma ask you, where's the shit at?"

"Bro, come on. Don't do this!" Flow pled.

Pow! Baby J popped him in the leg.

"Nigga, if you don't come with the answer, I'ma going to take it that ya want to do this the hard way!" Baby J yelled.

"It's in the back!" Flow quickly screamed.

"Go check, cuz," Baby J told Uno. Uno came back into the living room holding a small safe.

"It's fifty grand in there!" Flow said.

Uno looked at the safe and caught an attitude. "This all the fuckin' money you got?" Uno asked, slapping Flow across the face with his pistol.

"That's all of it!" Flow cried out as piss trickled down his leg.

"All this stunting your cousin is doing around the city, and all ya got is fifty put up? I should kill both of you niggas. Where the rest of the shit at, nigga?"

"It's all in the boxes around the kitchen and living room," Flow replied, holding pressure on his gunshot.

Uno started smiling when he looked into the box on the floor, and it was filled with fifteen pounds, and the next two had the same amount.

"Lay your bitch ass down!" Uno ordered, duct taping Flow's hands to his feet.

Uno and Baby J quickly moved the boxes to the door and grabbed the pounds off the table into another box. The more he thought about the lick, the happier he became. Uno grabbed all his money back up and stuffed it back into his bag. Looking out the peephole to make sure no one was looking or coming, Uno saw it was clear. They saw Flow trying to get loose. Walking over to Flow, Uno popped him in the kneecap, and that instantly made him cry out again.

"Thought we was out of here, huh?"

Flow looked up in their eyes and saw the boogie man.

Both Uno and Baby J pointed their guns at Flow and let them spark, lighting his ass up.

After Uno called everyone and told them he was getting a new number, he handed the homeless man sitting on the corner of 29th MLK the old phone and two hundred dollars.

"If you want to get on your feet, that's a come-up. I push weed," Uno said to the homeless man before speeding off.

Uno got back to the crib, put everything up, got fresh, and headed back out to celebrate his come-up.

Chapter 5

Punkin sat in the clinic, confused as to how she'd let Uno knock her up. She missed her time of the month. She sat in the house all weekend long, cleaning and pondering whether she was doing the right thing. After Uno got home, their relationship bloomed. She started crying every time she thought about their relationship because she was so in love with Uno.

Punkin nervously wiggled her fingers as she sat in the chilly, eerie room of the clinic. She called her little brother L when she woke up to talk to him, but after five minutes, he rushed her off the phone, saying he had to do something important, and he would see her when he came home.

Every time she tried to talk to Uno about being pregnant, she got scared of the response she would get. She had all types of things running through her head. They were both fourteen years old, too young to have kids. Uno always told her he wanted to build a big family with her.

"Punkin Walton?" a young, black nurse called out from a window.

Giving a warm smile, Punkin stood up. "Hi. I'm Walton," she said, walking up.

"Follow me, please," the nurse said, then led her to a back room.

Punkin slowly walked down the chilly hallway like it was the walk of shame. Her stomach did somersaults, and it felt like she could puke up her breakfast at any time. She didn't know if she was headed to do something important, and he would see her when he came home.

At that point, Uno was the only one who didn't know. Her mother told her she had to do something because she *wasn't taking care of no new baby.*

"You can have a seat on the table," the young nurse told Punkin.

"Relax. You seem like you're nervous," the nurse said, moving about the room.

"How you know?" Punkin asked with a smile.

"I see the way you keep moving," the nurse said, checking Punkin's blood pressure.

Punkin just nodded her head.

"It's goin' to be okay," the nurse said with a smile on her face. "I know this is a hard decision for you to make by yourself, so if you have an inch of doubt in your mind, you should take the time to think about it," the nurse said.

"Can you excuse me for a hot second while I make a call?"

The nurse just nodded in understanding.

"Thank you," Punkin said, then grabbed her purse and headed outside to place her call. While standing in front of the clinic, Punkin held her breath, waiting for Uno to pick up the phone.

"Hello?" Uno answered in a stern voice with a little attitude.

"Can we talk, or is this a bad time?" Punkin asked.

"Naw, baby, why would you say that. You can have all my time," Uno said, sitting up in bed.

"Well, I want you to know that I'm at the clinic, and I missed my time of the month, but momma told me I couldn't keep the baby and to do something about it, so I thought about getting an abortion."

"What? Y'all tripping, thinking y'all can do that without talking to me first. I want all my seeds," Uno said with attitude. "If you do that, I promise you, I'm goin' to kill all y'all," Uno said, hanging up the phone in Punkin's ear.

***

Harding was packed, as always, when Uno pulled up and parked in front of Butler's, where a small crowd was gathered outside. They stood around, conversing, while they smoked cigarettes and weed, and drank their drinks. Everyone seemed to enjoy the loud music that could be heard coming from someone's car. It had only been a week and a half since he and Baby J touched Flow, and he had fleeced over twenty pounds, not counting the last ten he was about to unload on his people.

It was a sunny Wednesday outside. When Uno grabbed his phone, he saw a group of females coming out of Butler's, looking at him, and that put a smile on his face. Uno headed inside to grab a bite to eat. He hit one with dap and shared head nods with the few hitters in the spot. He stood to the side so he could see the door.

After placing his order, Uno sat down and debated with himself on whether he should grab a trap since he didn't need to be in Gee's anymore. He was sitting on a little over a hundred thousand dollars, the most he'd ever had in his life. At the age of fourteen, Uno was making a name for himself and stepping out the shadows of his brother. If Ant knew Uno was moving around, he would be mad, whereas, on the other hand, Big Dawg would have been happy to see him standing on his own. Too bad, Big Dawg had to go to prison for a year.

By nightfall, Uno handled all his business in the streets, so he headed to pick up Punkin so they could head to the police auction. He was about to cop himself something nice. Even though it was nightfall, the auction was swarming with hitters trying to find something to pop out with. Uno stood next to Baby J, scooping out the various cars.

"Cuz, do you know what ya looking for?" Baby J leaned over and asked him in his ear.

"I'll know when I see it," Uno replied. Baby J was getting heated as he stood and watched car after car pass by.

"There her fine ass go!" Uno said as he walked over and inspected a Land Rover.

Baby J was relieved, then followed behind him. Uno popped the hood and let Baby J check to make sure everything was right so Uno could drive it off the lot. Baby J stepped back, smiled, and then threw both of his thumbs in the air.

"Get it!" Uno told Baby J. "I'm putting it in Momma's name."

Baby J walked off to find his female friend who worked at the auction so he could pay her off.

"I found one, baby," Uno told Punkin as she walked up to him and handed him a water. After cashing out, Uno drove off the lot in a new truck, with Baby J following him to the paint shop.

The next week, Uno smiled when he pulled up to the paint shop and saw his truck shining in the front. The sunlight beamed down mercilessly on the paint job, making it sparkle. He walked around, inspecting it for any flaws, and saw none. Everything looked pretty good to him, so he headed inside to pay the clerk the remaining two grand on his balance and grab his keys.

"So, what you think about your baby out there?" Pone asked him when he walked through the door of the shop.

"You did your thang," Uno told him, handing him his cash.

"Appreciate it," Pone said, handing over the keys.

Uno threw the keys to the rental to LR. "Follow me," he said.

LR was admiring Uno's whip as he drove down the street. He wanted to be like his brother. Uno came home and started doing good for himself. He didn't let the boy's school make him bitter.

Later that day, Uno filled his truck up and explored the city, getting his shine on. He watched everybody he passed try to see who was riding in that truck sitting on twenty-twos.

Chapter 6

For the past few weeks, Uno had been partying, hanging out, and blowing money. He was sexing so many women on the regular, he felt he never did a bid in boys' school.

Every day that passed, Uno found himself in the hottest spot, throwing money, showing out, and that was what got his name ringing in the streets as the young nigga to see. That was how he bagged the victim who lay next to him. He looked over her body and shook his head at the outline of the fine, thick specimen underneath the sheets.

Raven was what you called 'hood all around' from the way she walked, ate, talked, and hustled. She stood about five feet five, had a Hershey's complexion, gray eyes, a cute shape, and a short bob. She did everything she could to keep everything she needed. She used her body to trick men into paying her bills. Poverty was all she knew.

"Check out time is in thirty minutes," Uno said, shaking Raven. She sat up in bed, looking around while combing her fingers through her hair.

Twenty minutes later, Uno pulled into Sutton Place's outpost and let Raven out of the car. While out east, Uno decided to stop at the Washington Mall to see what new clothes were out. By twelve o'clock, Uno was headed to Punkin's job. It then dawned on him how little time he'd been spending with Punkin since getting home from boy school. He'd been so caught up dealing with females all over the city and partying that he had been neglecting the one he should've been giving the most attention. What put the icing on the cake was realizing he hadn't gotten on from Baby J or hustled in a few weeks. He made a mental note to himself to check his bankroll when he got home.

As Uno headed off the highway, he thought about Punkin and smiled. She was a good female, and he loved her like no other. She had a go-getter mentality like his, and that was one of the reasons he connected with her on a deeper level. She was just a female version of himself, and people had been telling him for a while. It was crazy that after he sexed females, he'd just go on about his business, but with Punkin, the sex was amazing, and then the conversation made it even better because they could joke and have fun.

Punkin was just walking out the front door of the restaurant, looking good in a Sequin Rosario outfit with the shades to match. Uno had gotten her some clothes when he went out of town on the weekend. She looked so good and innocent, to the point it made Uno feel worse for not spending time.

'I gotta get myself on the right track,' he said to himself, getting out to walk around so he could open the car door for Punkin.

After getting in the car, Punkin saw that Uno had been to the mall again. She couldn't do anything but roll her eyes at him.

"I see you been to the mall again, huh?" she commented.

"Ye-yea-yeah," Uno stuttered. Punkin rolled her eyes again. "Are you busy tonight again?"

"Naw, we can do whatever you wanna do," Uno said, smiling, thinking everything was good.

Irritated with Uno, Punkin just shook her head. It had been a few weeks since they'd been out to do anything. She decided it was time to enlighten Uno.

"You know, ever since you hooked up your car and started moving around, you changed up on me," she looked over into his eyes and said.

"What you mean by that?" Uno asked, lightweight mad. Punkin rolled her eyes.

"Everything is all about Uno!"

Uno couldn't argue with her. She was right to feel, however type of way. He had gotten so caught up in the lifestyle that he'd been neglecting not only Punkin but his family.

"Listen, baby. If I disrespected you in any kind of way, I truly apologize."

"You know I was in boys school for some time. I've just been enjoying all the stuff I missed out on, feel me. You don't know how it feels to be caged up, then let free."

"I can't say I understand, but I feel you, and you owe me," Punkin responded with a smile while rubbing her stomach.

"You got that," Uno said as he pulled up in front of her mother's crib. "Baby, call the movies and find us something late to go see. We'll go grab a bit to eat first, and then we'll catch the movie. How that sound?" he asked while leaning over to kiss her on the cheek.

"I'll call you and let you know what time the movie starts," she said, hopping out, smiling.

Uno sat and watched as she entered the house before pulling off, headed to the crib. The first thing Uno did when he entered the crib was head to his safe. He was in disbelief with the number, so he recounted it again carefully.

'Twenty thousand?' he said to himself. He was light-headed, and the room started spinning. He couldn't believe that, in two months, he'd blown over a hundred. He felt silly for killing Flow and not doing shit with the money. 'Easy come, easy go,' he thought to himself. He knew he'd gotten too caught up in the moment of thoughtless splurging. He knew he had to get back on the grind.

After cursing himself out, Uno hopped in the shower. Punkin called, and he and she agreed to dine at Jacqueline's Soul Food before catching a movie. It was a little past six o'clock, and the movie started at ten, so Uno was going to swing by Punkin's crib to pick her up around 7:30 p.m.

While in the shower, Uno had a lot of thoughts running through his mind. He had been out for two and a half months and had head-bodied someone for the first time. He could tell his cousin Baby J did that shit before; he needed to grab a crib because Punkin was doing a few months, and he wanted her to just focus on school and had been the best mother, and he was tired of having to use his brother's crib or spending money on hotels to sex females. He knew his mom and little sister would be mad, but he had to spread his wings a little. He would still keep his room.

"Hey, lil' fella. Let me holla at you for a minute!" Ant yelled for Uno when he came out of the front door.

Smiling, Uno swagged over to Ant's car. "What's up, big bro and cousin Bird?" he asked, giving the two dap.

"Have a seat in the car." They waited until Uno sat on the hood in between the two. Then Ant threw his hand on Uno's shoulder, and with a sincere look on his face, he said, "Bro, I'm worried about you. I been hearing a lot of shit, and I been watching shit, too. Lately, all I've been seeing is you around here, driving around in that truck with all these new clothes and jewelry. Nigga, your eyes. They don't have the same look they did when you stood before us on the porch."

Uno was all ears. *'Damn, had everyone seen it but me?'*

Ant continued. "I'm not goin' to keep you long, lil' bro, but I'ma leave you with this. See, I've been where you are! The spending, the women, the partying, and riding around. Money changes people—their presence, their attitudes, and their actions. If you goin' to be out here hustling, have a reason to hustle. Don't be out here doing it just to be doing it. Same shit we told Baby J. Y'all went away to boy school for years. Use what you learned in there. And from seeing me, Big Dawg, and Bird, apply it to yourself. You have principles that you live by. If you compromise those principles, then you will lose sight of who you are."

Uno sat in deep thought and let Ant's words sink in.

"Money comes and goes. You can get it, but the hardest part is keeping it," Ant said.

"Listen, lil' cuz. Use your head, and you'll go far. Surround yourself around positive and ambitious people, and you'll never go broke. Life is like chess, and every move you make can cost you. Always remember a fool acts on emotion, but a smart man thinks everything out," Bird said, pointing at his temple.

"Trust me, cuz. It works for us. Look at *us!*" Bird said, smiling, standing up. "Nigga, we've been having money for years, and that's because we've invested our money. Big Dawg is goin' to prison but still making money. You see, some people hustle for the fame and street cred, but when we was standing on the block, it was for you and Baby J, so ya'll didn't do this, but I guess it's in ya'll blood," Bird said.

"Thanks, big bro and cuz. I needed this talk," Uno said as he embraced one after the other. Uno saw the time. "I gotta go pick up Punkin. I'll see ya'll soon," he said, then walked over and hopped in his truck.

Ant waved at Uno as he sped off. He could've easily made a phone call and erased all of Uno's problems.

Chapter 7

A week had passed since Ant and Bird pulled down on Uno and had a pep talk with him. Ever since that day, Uno had fallen back on spending and gotten back to what he knew—grinding. Things were moving very slowly for Uno. For some reason, Uno felt like he was grinding for nothing. He needed his hands on a steady connect. His brothers wouldn't ever serve him, saying they weren't going to be the reason he got fucked. He was still grinding the weed, but lately, he had been copping a few ounces from different niggas around the hood to stay afloat.

Uno pulled into the Shell gas station on 38th and Capitol to fill up his truck. It was a bright, sunny, beautiful Saturday, and that day, he just wanted to cruise around the city, blowing some trees and getting his mind right. He was debating with himself on which city he wanted to hit because he was getting tired of the same thing every day.

"Damn, the city done changed a lot," Nasty said as he waited for the light to turn green. Nasty thought his eyes and mind were playing tricks on him. *'Damn, that nigga looks like Uno,'* he thought to himself, staring at the truck. "That is my nigga!" Nasty said, making a U-turn.

Meanwhile, numerous girls walked by, waving, flirting with Uno while he pumped his gas. When an unfamiliar H2 Hummer with dark tints pulled up beside him, he instinctively eased his .45 caliber off his waist.

Nasty hopped out of the truck and jokingly threw his hands in the air. "Damn, bro! Don't shoot!"

"Oh, shit, nigga! I thought you still had a few weeks?" Uno asked as the two embraced each other.

"I got out yesterday. Ms. Long got me out. God damn, nigga. You weren't playing no games, were you?" He walked around, inspecting Uno's Land Rover.

"I ain't on shit," Uno said like it was nothing.

Nasty nodded his head while checking out Uno's wardrobe and jewelry game. From the outside, looking in, Uno was executing his plan.

"So, damn, nigga, why you didn't pull up over mom's house yesterday?"

Nasty shrugged his shoulders. "I just went by and saw my kids, hit Ashley up for a shot, and then spent the rest of the day getting my mind right. I had a lot to think about."

"I feel you, Playboy," Uno said. Truthfully, hearing Ashley's name turned his stomach. Their boy school bid, all Ashley did was fuck Nasty.

"I know what you're thinking, bro."

Uno gave him a head nod. "Who whip you driving anyway?" Uno nodded his head toward the Hummer truck.

"That's Ashley's sister's baby daddy, Two-Tall. He be fucking with Man-Man from the hood," Nasty said.

Uno let out a laugh. "You talking about Pooh. Yeah, I know that chick. I was with her the other night," Uno said. "Anyway, where you laying your head at?" Uno asked Nasty.

"I'm chilling at Momma's crib, and yeah, my cousin told me you been creeping around with her since you been home." Nasty laughed.

Uno let out a laugh as well, but he was hot that Ashley talked his business, so he was going to call and cuss her ass out.

"I got that bread at the crib for you, too," Nasty said

"Cool. You know Punkin's pregnant now? She due in a few months."

"What? Punkin!" Nasty asked, laughing.

"Bro, we gotta get you out of those prison wear," Uno said, tagging on Nasty's pants.

"Well, follow me back over to the hood to drop dude's truck back off," Nasty said, hopping in the Hummer.

After dropping off the truck and swinging by the liquor store, Uno leaned back in the passenger seat while Nasty drove downtown to the mall.

As usual, on a Saturday, the mall was packed when they pulled into the parking garage. The two sat in the truck, puffing on a blunt Uno rolled while passing their bottle. A few minutes later, the two emerged from the car, eyes red with a nice buzz from the bottle.

"Here. Take this," Uno said, passing Uno five thousand dollars.

Nasty's face lit up. Not only had Uno split the bread before he left, but he was now giving him money to spend on clothes.

For the next two hours, Uno went from store to store, accumulating bag after bag. Nasty and Uno dressed totally differently from one another. Nasty loved nothing but hood shit, whereas Uno was a fly dude who could dress for any occasion. Uno just had this standout presence.

The two were having a ball until they walked into the food court and spotted something that altered their moods. Man-Man and his entourage mobbed through the entrance of the mall like they owned the world. Man-Man's name was ringing hard in the streets. Ever since Man-Man's cousin left him dope and spots, Man-Man had been getting money.

Man-Man's crew was decked out in the latest fashions from head to toe. Every girl's eyes were on them as their jewelry glistened as they walked through the mall. Uno gritted his teeth when he and Man-Man made eye contact. The two shared a personal beef.

"What's up, Uno and Nasty? Y'all need to get y'all weight up because that little spendin' y'all just did is what we throw in parties," Man-Man said with a sarcastic smirk on his face when he walked by.

Man-Man's crew sized up Uno and Nasty and smiled as they walked off. Nasty held Uno back from getting at Man-Man. "Chill out, bro! Fuck them niggas! We gonna get our time!" Nasty said as they watched Man-Man and his crew mob through the mall, deep.

"Let's get up outta here," Uno said as they both stormed toward the entrance.

Uno's mind seemed distant as he headed into the city.

"You know I really appreciate the love, bro," Nasty said over the Yung Joc CD.

Uno snapped out of his daze. "We family, nigga! That's how family supposed to take care of theirs. Ant got a stash for you, too."

The two drove in silence for a moment before Nasty broke the silence.

"Lil' bro, I gotta get my hustle on," Nasty said, taking a sip from the bottle. You know how a nigga feel when they money ain't right. Shit, bro. I'm thinking about hollering at this one nigga Hip-Hop that Ashley fucks with to see if he would hit me off. Shit, I thought about gettin' at his ass," Nasty said.

The two laughed.

"Who the nigga fucks with anyways?" Uno asked.

"I think them nigga's Man-Man," Nasty said, eyeing Uno.

With an idea popping in his mind, Uno rubbed his chin and said, "I wonder if the nigga got some weight?"

"Call Ashley and tell her you tryna holla at him!" Uno told him as he took a few pulls from the blunt and exhaled a cloud of smoke.

"What you tryna cop, bro?" Nasty asked when Uno handed him his phone.

"Shit, I want to cop two bricks," Uno lied. "But I'll cop a few ounces off him first to see if it do what it supposed to do. Then if it's A-1, I'll get back wit' him on the up and up."

After Ashley asked 101 questions about how he got so much money so fast when he was only recently getting home. Ashley ended up hooking up a meeting between Hip-Hop and Nasty for seven o'clock.

Later that night, the two met up with Hip-Hop and copped a few ounces off him. Uno gave Ashley a few hundred dollars for making the transaction at her parents' crib and went to drop the work off at his mom's crib. Then he and Nasty went out searching for some new pussy. Within the hour, they were headed to a hotel with two fine ass females.

***

Punkin promptly arrived at Uno's mom's spot at 9:30 a.m. with the rental car he had requested. She stood on the porch and rang the doorbell.

"I'm coming!" Uno yelled, hopping out of the shower, wet.

Punkin folded her arms, sucked her teeth, and pouted when he opened the front door. "I thought you were gonna be ready to go."

"Just give me one minute," he said, kissing her before leaving her standing in the living room while he went back into the bathroom.

Punkin sat down in the loveseat. While she waited for Uno, she gazed over at all the family pictures on the entertainment center, which she always did when she was at the house. Uno's little sister and cousin Baby J resembled Ant so much that you would have thought they were brother and sister.

"It's time to get your own place!" she yelled to Uno.

"I'm working on that now!" he yelled from his bedroom door. "Why you so worried about me gettin' my own crib?" he asked when he walked into the living room.

"'Cause I would like to get my fuck on at your place and not here, your sister's, or a hotel," Punkin said.

Uno smiled. "I'll tell you what, then. Since you so in a hurry for me to break your back in, in my own spot, that's your little assignment. Find me a place."

"Fine then," Punkin said, grabbing her purse as they both headed for the front door.

Uno hopped in his truck, and Punkin followed him out to a storage unit on the south side. Realizing how silly it was to blow through all that money in a few months, Uno had Punkin's auntie rent a storage unit to put his truck up for the time being. He was staying two steps ahead, knowing he was about to get to the money. He didn't want his truck to be hot. After parking his truck in the unit and locking it up, he hopped in with Punkin.

Dropping Punkin off at her cousin's crib, LR ran out of the house and jumped into the car, and the two headed to the hood to get on the grind. As he cruised through the hood, he just shook his head at how much had changed. The hood had flipped over, and all kinds of new faces were hugging the block. It wasn't full of life like when Ant, Bird, and Big Dawg were standing out here. Although a little money still rolled around the hood, most of the money went to Hip-Hop. The word on the street was that Man-Man was supplying Hip-Hop with rocks so big that other niggas couldn't compete. The only clientele who remained loyal to the ones in the head were the ones who'd been staying there for years, but even some of them went and copped from Hip-Hop.

Uno was on a mission to get it rocking. He didn't care what the next nigga was doing, because he was too focused on himself. He'd been taught by the best, and it was time to put his skills to work.

That entire day, Uno and LR made their rounds, giving everybody testers so word could spread that they were back in the hood. As he posted up on Udell, he stared at the house they used to stay in back in the day. He thought about when they had a Shrimp Hut on the corner, and he reminisced on all the good times he, Nasty, and a few others shared. It felt good to be in the hood. He smiled as the whole scenery brought back so many vivid memories. He took a swing out of the bottle and puffed on the blunt he was blowing as he and LR walked down Udell.

Uno felt a funny feeling wash over his body as a cool breeze came through and ruffled his shirt. He smiled and looked down at the chain and ring he got from Big Dawg. He glanced up at the sky and said a silent prayer.

By nightfall, Uno and LR had made over five thousand and felt content with their first day out there.

"Big bro, I'm tryin got be out here wit' you every day," LR said, counting the money Uno gave him.

Utilizing everything he had learned from Ant, Big Dawg, Bird, and the streets, it didn't take long for Uno to build up his clientele. In a few weeks, Uno and LR had Udell jumping like the old days. Money was coming in from all angles. Traffic flowed through the hood like it was a detour route.

Uno fulfilled Punkin's wish by pulling up in a truck and telling her it was time to move. He had found himself an apartment on High School Road, out west. Thanks to the crackheads from the hood, he was able to furnish his entire apartment and still cop a few bricks.

With things looking up for Uno and with Punkin's birthday only a few days away, he had a few tricks he was putting together.

Chapter 8

A few days later, Uno had to get up at the crack of dawn to prepare for Punkin's birthday. Although she wasn't due to arrive home until later in the day, he still wanted to make sure everything was perfect for her. It was rare to find someone as special as Punkin.

Uno's first stop that morning was to Tiffany's jewelry store, where he picked up a karat solitaire diamond ring he had custom-made, along with a three-karat tennis bracelet. Victoria's Secret was the next stop. There, he purchased a few lingerie sets, along with a few bottles of body wash. He smiled to himself as he watched the cashier gift wrap everything he got, excited by the thought of Punkin stripping out of one of the lingerie sets for him.

Uno left the mall and headed straight to Build-A-Bear, where he purchased roses, rose petals, one human-sized bear, and several different colored balloon bouquets. To add to the decor, he even purchased blue silk sheets.

The minute Uno arrived at their crib, he immediately went to work decorating. He started in the bedroom by changing the room around, then switching his sheets with the silk ones he purchased.

Next, he sprinkled rose petals all over the bed and throughout the room, all the way into the hallway. He made sure he made the rose petals lead from the front door to the bubble bath he was going to have waiting. After he finished, he nodded his head in admiration and then checked his

Rolax. It was a little past five p.m., and Punkin was getting off work, so that gave Uno over an hour before she arrived.

Uno headed into the kitchen, washed his hands, and immediately slapped the pork chops on the counter and into the batter, then threw them in the oven. Just like everyone else in his family, he was a master at cooking. He already had the sauce for the chops ready, along with the whole potatoes, mac and cheese, and a nice salad.

Once dinner was completed, Uno set the table, lit a couple of candles, and then set the salad and a bottle of chilled champagne in the middle of the table. He covered the food and rushed to hop in the shower. While Uno showered, he smiled to himself. He couldn't wait to see the look on Punkin's face when she walked through the door.

'I'm the truth,' he thought to himself. After slipping on a pair of silk Polo pajamas, Uno squirted on a little Polo Blue and surveyed the room. Lighting the candles around the house to give it that smell, mixed with the food, he put the bracelet on the bear's arms and set the ring on its lap.

Meanwhile, Punkin was climbing up the stairs and sniffing the air. "Damn, somebody's throwing down," she said. The more she climbed, the stronger the aroma got. Punkin smiled when she made it to the top and realized the aroma was coming from their apartment.

"This nigga thinks he the truth," she said, out of breath.

"Damn, it smells good out here," the couple that stayed next door to them said.

"Thank you, and hello. I'm Punkin. We moved in next door," Punkin said.

"I'm Martha, and this my husband, Shawn," Martha said, reaching out to shake Punkin's hand.

"When are y'all due, and do you know what y'all having?" Shawn asked.

"We'll be having a girl, and I'm due in a few months," Punkin responded while rubbing her stomach.

Uno heard Punkin's voice, so he inspected the house on last time, smiled, and then headed to the front door. He waited for Punkin to knock because she never took her keys. She knocked extra hard.

"Who this at my door?" Uno asked jokingly.

"Boy, you better stop playing and open this damn door!" Punkin yelled.

"Alright, damn, but take them shoes off," Uno demanded. Punkin knew not to play with Uno, so she pouted while taking off her shoes.

When Uno finally moved out the way, she threw her hands over her mouth and said, "Oh my God! Who did this?"

"Go ahead, baby! Walk on them," Uno said as he stepped to the side to let Punkin step on the rose petals.

Once she stepped inside, he directed her toward the beautiful candlelit dinner table. "After you, sexy," he said.

"You the truth," Punkin said as Uno pulled out her chair for her to sit. Punkin sat back and stared in admiration while Uno moved throughout the kitchen, heating up dinner and preparing their plates.

"Here you are," Uno said, placing her plate in front of her.

"Wow! Mm, these are good," she said after taking a bite of her chops.

Uno popped the cork on the bottle of Don P, poured himself a glass, and poured her some water. "I'd like to propose a toast."

Punkin smiled and lifted her glass.

"To your fifteenth birthday," he said, and the two clanked their glass.

For the next hour, they giggled and talked while Uno romantically fed Punkin.

"Mm, that was good," she said.

After cleaning up their messes, Uno reached out for Punkin's hand. "Come with me," he said, then led her down the hallway to his bedroom. It looked like they were headed down the altar.

When Punkin walked through the bedroom door, all she could do was smile upon seeing the bubble bath with a single white rose and lace lingerie set sitting on top of the counter next to a big, puffy towel.

"Baby, I want you to relax because today is your day," he said, helping her undress. He then helped her into the bath.

"Ahh, mm," Punkin said as she immersed her body into the water.

Uno grabbed the sponge, kneeled before her, and started bathing Punkin. He couldn't resist sucking and licking her neck.

"God damn, baby. That feels so good" She moaned. "Can't you wait until we get into the bedroom?" she asked, rubbing his back.

Uno smiled. "Okay, baby, but this is to be continued," he replied, grabbing the wash rag and beginning to wash her up. After washing her, he helped her stand while he grabbed the towel and set it near.

"Go 'head and finish," he said, patting her on the butt.

'He's crazy,' she said to herself, smiling as she finished washing her ass and pussy, then dried off and slipped into the lingerie set. She looked at herself in the mirror.

There was a trail of rose petals leading to the bedroom when Punkin came out of the bathroom. She smiled as she slowly followed them. She couldn't believe her eyes when she entered the bedroom. Staring in amazement, she placed her hand on her chest. She felt so good at that moment that tears poured down her cheeks. She looked at Uno stretched out across the bed in his silk boxers.

He motioned for her with his finger. "All this is for you, baby," he said, smiling. "Here is our third wheel," he said, handing out the bear.

Punkin smiled as she cheerfully saw the Tiffany bracelet around the arm of the bear.

"Keep looking, baby," Uno said.

When Punkin saw the ring hanging off the tennis bracelet, she damn near lost it. "Oh my God!" Uno had touched her so deeply that she felt like she had gone to heaven. Punkin jumped out of her underwear, eased onto the bed, and started smothering Uno with kisses. "I love you, baby!"

Lying Punkin down, Uno eased on top of her. "It's your night. I'm the one that's supposed to be kissing all over your body," he said with a laugh before he started planting soft kisses all over her.

Hopping up fast and scared, Punkin, as she watched Uno walk over to the flowers that sat on the dresser and took a single rose. He turned the CD player on, and Keith Sweat came blasting through the speakers.

Uno was already disappearing under the sheets, and he started skillfully licking her body while trailing it with the rose. Punkin moaned and squirmed as she rubbed the back of his head. Uno licked around her navel, then worked his way up to her breasts and kissed both of them equally. With her being pregnant, her nipples swelled. Uno came up from under the sheet.

"Aww, baby, you're the best," Punkin took the rose and said, smelling it.

Uno didn't respond as he slowly descended to her love box. Her eyes got as big as apples when he started massaging her clit with his tongue.

"Oh, shit, baby!" she cried out with her mouth open as his fingers went to work, going in and out. She almost lost it when Uno applied pressure to a magical spot inside her pussy walls. Feeling like she had to piss, Punkin started to push him off so she could get up, but Uno grabbed her legs and locked them around his head as he sucked hard.

"Baby, oh, shit! I feel like I have to piss!" Punkin said, not able to hold it back. Punkin stared down at Uno's face and the puddle beneath them.

"I'm just getting started," Uno said, taking out his fingers and sucking her juice off them. "Mm. Damn, baby, you taste good," he said, staring into her eyes.

Punkin was in a daze. Uno was really turning her on by licking her juices off his fingers. She didn't know what had just happened to her, because she had never experienced it.

Punkin flinched as Uno ran his tongue up her clit, parting her lips with his tongue. Moving his tongue around her clit had every hair on her body at attention. Uno's lick and suck combinations had Punkin feeling like she was on cloud nine. Her body went into convulsions when she looked down at him and watched him slowly slide her pussy lips in his mouth. Two orgasms later, Uno came up with pussy juice all over his face again.

"You ready for the real thing?" he asked.

Punkin lay in the bed in a daze, trying to catch her breath. "Oh my God!" she said for the fourth time, gasping for air. Her body just kept shaking.

Uno slowly kissed her neck while he eased inside her.

Punkin flinched a little. "Uno, slow!"

He kissed her on the forehead and then eased a little more of himself inside her.

"Umm." Punkin moaned in his ear.

Thanks to the foreplay, she was extremely wet. The more Uno eased inside her, the harder she started to breathe. The more he filled her walls up, the more her juices overflowed out of her pussy and onto the bed. Before long, Punkin was matching Uno's pace.

"Who pussy is this?" Uno asked, performing slow, deep, hard strokes.

Punkin moaned in ecstasy.

"Let me know it's mines," Uno said, digging deeper and stroking faster.

Punkin bit his chest. "Oh, shit, baby. It's yours. It's yours!" She moaned loudly. The more they sexed, the hotter it got in the room. Both bodies had rose petals stuck to them.

He pumped and pumped as he felt the tingling he knew too well. Releasing his hot sperm inside her, Uno's head spun.

The two came together in unison and squeezed each other tightly. Punkin's body couldn't stop shaking as Uno lay on top of her with his dick still inside of her cavity.

"That was amazing," Uno whispered in her ear as he rolled off her.

For the next few minutes, she rested her head on Uno's chest, listening to his heartbeat while engaging in a conversation. He was a good listener, giving her his undivided attention.

After letting Punkin talk, Uno took her into his arms. "Time to go again," he said.

By the end of the night, the two had worked their way around the apartment and then ended the memorable night, falling asleep on top of roses and in each other's arms. The next morning, Uno handed Punkin a .22.

Chapter 9

When Uno and LR pulled up in the hood, crackhead Holla-Holla ambushed the car.

"Damn, baby, where y'all been? You've been missing out on money like crazy," Holla-Holla stressed with a couple of bills in her hand.

"I had to drop my BM off at work," Uno said, grabbing his pistol and hopping out of the car.

"Come on, boy," Holla-Holla said as she made her way toward her house. After serving Holla-Holla, Uno stepped out on the block and made some rounds. Cutting through the park and messing with some of the kids that were playing, he then handed out dollar bills.

"Thank you! You just like Ant and them!" some of the kids chanted when Uno walked off.

That entire day, money poured in from all angles. From the time Uno pulled up in the hood, his phone rang nonstop.

"Damn, shit is popping today, Big Bro!" LR said, going to grab another one out of their spot.

It had been less than two hours since Uno and LR came out of the house, and they were already sitting on five thousand.

The whole time Uno was grinding, he couldn't stop thinking about the night he had with Punkin. He knew Punkin wanted a commitment, but with him just coming home and being young, he was scared because he never knew what commitment meant. He knew Punkin was worth being with for the rest of his life.

By three o'clock that evening, they were down to a few grams, and judging by the way the hood was jumping, they knew they'd be out of dope soon. It made Uno shitty when he called Hip-Hop to find out he was waiting to re-up.

"I can't believe this shit. Friday, and it's jumping like this, and I run out of dope," Uno said after hanging up the phone with Hip-Hop.

Just then, both his and LR's phones went off with texts, and after looking down at their phones, they both smiled. It was their people from out south, asking to spend. Before they headed out south, Uno swung by Holla-Holla's crib and left her a few rocks to hold her for the night. Uno called Nasty to ask if he wanted to hold the rental because he wanted to bring out his truck for the night.

After serving their southside clientele, Uno and LR made a few stops before riding out to Nasty's mom's to scoop him.

When Uno pulled up, Nasty was on the porch with a bottle in his hand. Seeing Uno come down the street, Nasty locked up his mom's house and hopped in the ride. As soon as Nasty sat down in the car, Uno threw him a bag of weed and a couple of blunts for him to roll up. LR didn't smoke, so he didn't know how to roll.

As they traveled around the city, the three talked and brought each other up to speed on their lives. By the time they finished the two blunts, they were arriving at the storage unit. Uno hopped inside his truck, followed by LR, and inhaled the car air freshener. After backing out and locking up the storage unit, he hit his horn at Nasty, turned up Pac, and headed toward his apartment.

The minute they entered Uno's apartment, he began to strip out of his clothes because he was desperately in need of a hot shower.

As he headed to the bathroom, LR headed to the kitchen to grab something to eat.

When the hot water hit Uno's body, the tension escaped from it. He stayed in the shower until the water turned cold, then he hopped out and dried off. As he walked into his bedroom, his cell phone sounded off back-to-back, letting him know he had waiting texts, so he looked at the number.

'Who the fuck? 765-268-2181 #1000?'

His phone sounded again. This time, the display read *'765-268-2181 #911'*. He knew by the 765 that the caller was from one of the surrounding cities. What really caught his attention was the thousand behind the number, which meant someone was trying to spend a thousand with him.

"Let me find out who the fuck this is," he said, dialing the number on his cell phone.

"Hello?"

"Who the fuck is dis?" Uno asked.

"What's up? This is Dawn. Can you hook me?"

Uno looked at his phone at the time. *Damn!* He and Punkin were catching the 9:30 p.m. movie, and it was going on at 8:30 p.m.. He knew it would be hard to make the run and get back in time. He resonated with himself that he could hit the hallway and make it back in time. Besides, a thousand-dollar sale wasn't something you just missed.

"Fuck! Damn!" Uno cursed, remembering that Nasty had the rental for the night.

"So what's up? Are you coming?" Dawn impatiently asked.

Uno rubbed his head while pacing the floor. He had to contemplate for a minute, then asked, "Where you at?"

"I'm in Anderson, on Main Street."

"Damn. Alright. I'll be there in thirty minutes," he said.

"Okay, I'll see you then, baby," Dawn said, then hung up the phone.

Uno grabbed the little stash he had left and counted the rocks he had in the bag. All he had left was twenty-five nice-sized dubs.

"I know what I'ma do," Uno said to himself, then immediately started breaking down the twenty-five. When he finished, he had fifty nice-sized rocks.

"Thousand dollars? Yeah, she'll go for this," he said as he held the rock up in the air. Uno grabbed his keys, cell, and a few blunts. "I be back, lil' bro," Uno said to LR as he bounced out the door. "Damn, I'ma gonna stick out in this truck," he said while hopping in.

***

When Uno turned down Main Street, he immediately spotted Dawn standing in front of her house. He pulled into a parking spot, looked at her, nodded his head, parked, and then walked over to her. He surveyed the block before making a beeline toward her.

"Hey, boo," Dawn said, then anxiously handed him ten crisp hundred-dollar bills.

A suspicious-looking dude standing off to the side made Uno hesitate in handing her the rocks. "Who the fuck is dude?" he asked.

"Oh, he's just one of my tricks," Dawn replied.

"I told you when you were in the city that I wasn't trying to meet no new faces," Uno said. He cautiously looked around the area before grabbing the bag of rocks and handing them to her.

"Can I call you later on?" Dawn asked as Uno walked back toward his truck.

"Yeah. Next time, be by yourself," he replied, then hopped into the truck.

Dawn waved. "Bye, Uno! See you later, sweetie."

Uno pulled out onto the road and blended into traffic while nervously surveying the area, expecting to see police cars popping out. Uno let out a sigh of relief and smiled when he saw the road was free of police. When Uno pulled up to a stoplight, he glanced in his rearview mirror and noticed a police car behind him with the officer on his walkie-talkie. He eased off when the light turned green. He only made it a block away before the officer hit his lights. All Uno could do was shake his head.

"License and registration, please, sir?" the officer asked when he walked up.

As Uno handed over the requested information, he noticed an unmarked car pulling up.

"I'll be right back, sir," the officer said, walking off toward his police cruiser.

"I can't believe this bull," Uno said. Looking through his rearview, Uno tried to read the officer's body language as he walked back toward the car.

"Is everything okay, officer?" Uno asked with a smile on his face.

"Sir, I'm gonna have to ask you to step out of the car."

"For what?" Uno asked.

"Sir, again, could you please just step out the car?" the officer asked, taking a step back with his hand on his gun.

"This is some bullshit," Uno mumbled as he exited his car.

"What the hell's going on?" Uno asked when he noticed the tow truck pulling up behind them.

"Can you please walk to the back of the truck?" the officer asked.

Doing as the officer instructed, Uno shook his head as he walked around toward the back.

"I'm gonna need you to place your hands on the truck and spread your legs for me."

'Glad I left my 9mm at the crib tonight,' Uno thought while getting shook down.

"This is quite a bit of money you have here, sir. Where do you work?" the officer asked as he set the pile of money on the roof.

'What the fuck is all this?' Uno wondered. He couldn't believe he let himself get caught slipping like this. The few thousand he had on him was the money he was goin' to give to Punkin to put up for them.

"Here we go!" the officer said, holding the ten hundred-dollar bills he'd just gotten from down in the air for whoever was sitting in the tinted unmarked car to see.

Both doors to the unmarked opened, and two males in plain clothes got out.

"What the fuck is this?" Uno asked.

"Sir, you are under arrest," the officer said, grabbing his cuffs.

"For what?" Uno spun around and asked, already knowing.

"You're under arrest for dealing and possession of crack," the officer said, spinning him back around and cuffing him.

"How the—" Uno's sentence was cut short when the officer spun him back around toward the unmarked car.

"Remember me?" the driver asked. Uno couldn't do anything but drop his head. *'I'ma kill that hoe!'* It turned out the guy whom Dawn said was her trick ended up being an undercover cop.

"We're seizing your truck since your car was used in the commission of a drug transaction. We're also seizing all the money, unless you have proof you work for this," the officer said with a smirk on his face.

The officer walked Uno toward his cruiser and placed him in the back seat.

Uno's stomach tightened as he watched his car get towed away.

'Damn, I told myself I would never get locked up again,' he thought.

Since Uno would be turning sixteen in a few months, they booked him into Anderson County Jail and held him on a hundred-thousand-dollar bond. Once fingerprinted, he had a free call to make. He phoned Punkin, who went crazy when she picked up the phone. After he calmed her down, Uno told her everything he needed her to do.

Immediately, Punkin asked to borrow her mother's car and shot out the door, making the rounds and gathering all she needed to get Uno's bond paid.

As Punkin put things together, Uno paced the cage he was in. Since it was night, he knew he wouldn't be bonded out until the wee hours. He sat down, resting his head against the wall. He couldn't believe he was once again sitting in the same place he promised himself he wouldn't go—jail. That entire night, he couldn't do anything but think about the steps he'd made to land him back there. He knew he should have listened to his instincts, but greed had gotten the better of him.

"Fuck!" Uno yelled, jumping off the bench.

Ten thousand gone, his truck gone, and not to mention, he had a legal situation. Not only that, but he still had to pay his bond and get a lawyer.

"As of today, I swear, by any means, I'm going to make every move I make a big one!" he said. *This is my last time I'ma let them put cuffs on me because I will hold court in the streets next time,'* he thought to himself as he went to lie down on the bench before he dozed off.

***

The next morning, Uno was awakened by the officer sliding open the cell door. "Brandon, you're free!" the officer said.

Uno sat up, stretched out, and wiped the sleep out of his eyes. After being processed for release, he walked out of the building to Punkin's mom's car. He got teary-eyed when he saw Punkin balled up in the driver's side with her coat over her face.

"You have a good woman on your hands. She's been waiting here since last night," the officer who let him outside said.

Uno knocked on the car window, waking Punkin up. Punkin smiled when she saw Uno standing there. Opening the door, she jumped into his arms. Uno smiled back and kissed her on the forehead.

"Oh, baby, you had me so scared."

Uno let a small laugh out. "Don't worry. I'ma be alright," he said, then threw his arm around her for a big hug.

The minute Uno entered their apartment, he started making calls, trying to search for a good lawyer. After he was done, he had a number for Hennessy, an aggressive lawyer known for beating cases. Uno talked with Hennessy's receptionist and scheduled an appointment, then headed to the bathroom to freshen up. Uno knew he was going to be spending a nice piece of change when he pulled up to Hennessy's office and saw her Ferrari parked out front.

When Uno walked through the front door, he thought he was walking into a five-star hotel, so he had to double-check he was in the right building. After making sure he was in the right spot, he made his way to the secretary's desk.

"Hello, my name is Brandon. I called a while ago to make a two o'clock appointment," Uno said.

The secretary picked up the phone, said a few words, and hung up. "Have a seat, sir," she said, eyeing Uno.

A mixed female came out of an office in her expensive, custom-made designer pantsuit and shook Uno's, Punkin's, and her aunt's hands.

During the introduction, Uno's eyes were looking over the woman's expensive timepiece and diamond necklaces. Her white teeth contributed to the effectiveness of her smile, and he knew those whites cost a pretty penny.

Hennessy led the group into her office, where she sat down in an extremely plush chair. Uno scanned Hennessy's decorated office. She had pictures with actors, athletes, politicians, and family members.

"Umm hmm. Uhh. Damn. Ahh," was all Hennessy mumbled, looking over the case. After looking over the file, all Hennessy could do was shake her head.

"Sir, we have good and bad news. Which one would you like to hear first?" Hennessy asked.

"Shit, gimme the bad," Uno said.

"The bad news is that a CI—confidential informant—and an undercover cop were present when the transaction was made, and knowing the prosecutors on your case will try to send you to prison—even though this is your first time—you're facing forty years, and with the witnesses, the case is even stronger."

"Damn," Uno replied, dropping his head. "Well, what's the good?" Uno asked, picking up his head.

"The good news is, I see some strong points I can argue."

Uno smiled. That was music to his ears.

"Can I speak with him alone, please?" Hennessy asked Punkin and her auntie.

Punkin looked at Uno for the okay, who nodded his head, and they excused themselves from the office.

After they left the office, Hennessy leaned forward and whispered, "No witness, no case." Then she calmly sat back in her chair.

Uno looked at Hennessy, who had a stern look on her face. He nodded his head in understanding of Hennessy's point.

"How much does a case like this cost?"

"For a case like this, you're looking to drop between ten and fifteen thousand," Hennessy said.

Uno rubbed his head. "You got a payment plan?"

Hennessy leaned forward again. "How much you have right now?"

"I'ma be honest with you. With them taking my car, my money, and me making bond, all I have to my name is a few thousand right now. But if you give me a few weeks, I can have the whole thing for you."

Hennessy looked down at the calendar on her desk.

"Can you have the rest by New Year's? That way, it gives you a few more months to get yourself together."

"I sure can," Uno said, nodding his head.

"Okay, I'll take your case. Did you bring that few thousand with you today?" Hennessy asked with a raised brow.

Uno smiled. "Yeah, I got it."

Hennessy cheerfully came from behind her desk, shook Uno's hand, and patted him on the back. "Don't worry yourself. You just hired the best lawyer in the city," she said with a smile. "I'm giving you 'til New Year's because I have a trial coming up in a few weeks that I have to prepare for. You might know Baby J?" she commented to see if he did.

"Yeah, that's my cousin," Uno replied with a smile, exited the office, and stopped by the secretary's desk to pay the few thousand.

As he drove home, he had all types of thoughts running through his head. He was sad because he knew his car and the money he'd grinded so hard for were gone. Plus, he didn't know his cousin was fighting a case.

"You gonna be alright, baby," Punkin said as he looked over and saw the stress on Uno's face.

***

Uno felt better after Punkin helped him release all of the tension he had built up inside him. Love making always seemed to temporarily get people's minds off their problems. He felt like he was always on cloud nine when he was inside Punkin.

He looked down at her sleeping peacefully on his chest. She was an angel. "I love you, baby," he said, kissing her face.

'*He had hit the bottom*,' he thought as he stared up at his ceiling. Although he was at the bottom, at least he was still free to do as he pleased. His birthday and Christmas were around the corner, so he had to pick himself up and come up with a plan because bills were coming in, and he still had to pay Hennessy her money. Looking at his gun, he knew what he had to do. After coming up with a plan, he kissed Punkin on the forehead, hugged her tight, and called it a night.

Chapter 10

For the past few months, Uno couldn't catch a break to save his life. It seemed like he was catching pure hell since getting hit with that case. After pawning everything he owned, he walked away with less than ten thousand, and that was only half of what he paid. Punkin had offered to give him her savings and to pawn her jewelry, but there was no way he could let her do that. He was grinding, but every time he turned around, something always came up.

The year was officially out the door. Things weren't going as Uno had planned. His Christmas had been horrible since he couldn't really get his family anything. His New Year's was terrible, his birthday was even more horrible, and then Valentine's Day came around, and it tore him up that he had to get a booster to grab something for Punkin. The only light his life had was a few days after Valentine's Day when Punkin pushed out his first child.

That was the month before. The day was then March first, and Uno was going to make that month better than his last ones. The hood had gotten so hot. Nasty and LR fucked up a few ounces, his clientele out South had moved out of town to get clean, and his plug was in the county.

It took Uno months to track down Dawn. Being a crackhead, she bounced from place to place, but his nigga Lil' Rube from Anderson had seen her and kept eyes on her, so that night, she would be residing at the H&K hotel.

Dressed in all black, Uno and Baby J blended into the dark alley, watching all the activity going on inside Dawn's hotel room. Things couldn't have been more perfect for them. The undercover cop and Dawn were the reason both Uno and Baby J were fighting for their lives. They'd been going around the city, setting people up.

They sat back and watched through Dawn's hotel window. The two were so gone that they never realized that their party was for all to see. Baby J and Uno watched them take turns feeding their noses with cocaine. Uno surveyed the area, while Baby J kept an eye on the sleazy hotel. Dawn's room was in the back of the lot on the first floor.

Baby J and Uno looked at each other, thinking the same thing. These were the only two people who could get them off the streets, so no matter what, they had to be dealt with, and that night was their night.

Staying close to the wall, they threw on their masks. The closer they got to Dawn's room, the louder the music became. The music really worked in their favor. They looked around one last time when they got to Dawn's room door before peeking inside. Dawn and the undercover cop hit more lines while sitting at the table. He looked through the window one last time to see where the two were. Giving Baby J a nod, he kicked in the door. The music was so loud that they never heard anything or saw the two masked men storm inside.

The undercover cop had his nose to the table when the two came in, but once he looked up, Uno dumped two shells inside his head. Blood dripped out of both holes as he fell back, collapsing on the floor.

"The dope and money is in the top dresser!" Dawn cried.

"This is much more than a robbery," Baby J stated, removing his mask.

Dawn almost passed out when she saw Baby J's and Uno's faces.

They both smirked. "You wasn't expecting to see our faces until you got on the stand?" Uno asked.

"I swear they made me do it! They been having us set people up," she said.

Baby J grabbed Dawn by the throat and slid his knife across her neck as her eyes popped out. "Now it's your turn to sleep," Baby J said in her ear as he let her body hit the floor. With the key witnesses dead, Uno and Baby J knew they were free men. Throwing their hoodies on, they both eased out of the hotel undetected.

"Be easy, lil' cuz," Baby J said, going his way.

"Love, cuz, and you do the same," Uno said, disappearing into the dark.

Being cautious not to be seen, Uno slipped back into his apartment and found Punkin still sleeping with Pooder on her chest. He grabbed the baby and put her inside her baby bed, then eased himself beside Punkin.

'Punkin is going to be my alibi,' he thought to himself as he fell asleep, cuddling with Punkin.

Chapter 11

Ever since the murders, Uno had been lying low, and with him lying low for the past week, his pockets had been hurting. *'I can't keep goin' for this shit. Something has to give,'* Uno thought as he stared at the television.

"Breaking news. We are deeply sorry to bring you this news from Anderson, Indiana, at the H & K hotel."

Uno sat up and turned the television up. Knowing what he knew, he had to hear what they were talking about.

"We, the police department, saw one of our own violently killed, along with a witness who was supposed to take the stand for the state. We are now connecting dots with Indianapolis because the witness was also supposed to be helping the police department there. We deeply understand how important it is for our residents in Anderson and Indianapolis to feel safe within our neighborhoods. If you have any information that would help lead us to who's done this, please call the number at the bottom of the television," Police Superintendent Coffee said.

Uno sat back with a smile on his face.

Meanwhile, Punkin was moving around the kitchen, preparing their dinner. Seeing Uno staring at the television concerned her. He hadn't been himself, and whenever she tried to talk to him, he would just blow it off. He always seemed like he was in a different world. Lately, she'd catch him just staring off into space.

'Something is wrong with my man, and I'm going to find out what it is that he has on his mind,' she said to herself,

walking into the living room. "Baby, what's on your mind?" she asked, plopping down into Uno's lap.

"I'm good," Uno lied, still watching the Bucks beat the Heat's ass.

"Talk to me, baby. I know there's something wrong with you," Punkin said with caring eyes.

"There's nothing to talk about. I'm straight. I will handle it myself," Uno said with an attitude.

"Well, how the hell you know I can't be a help?"

"Look, Punkin. Not right now, please," Uno said, easing her off his lap. He knew he had a big problem on his hands, and that was not having money.

"Listen, Uno. You're gonna talk to me one way or another," Punkin said, standing in front of the TV. "Baby, I don't like seeing you around here, dragging around the house, just staring off into space. If I didn't know no better, I would've thought you lost your dog. You ain't even been around my brother, Nasty, or any of my cousins. So I know something's wrong," Punkin said.

Uno twisted his face and just stared straight at her.

Punkin walked over to him and grabbed his face. "We've always been able to sit back and talk about any and everything… and now you're cutting me out like I haven't been the one on the up and up with you," Punkin said with tears rolling down her face.

"Look, Punkin, I'm just stressing! It's a lot going on! You gotta feel me. Just a few months ago, I had a nice amount of money, a car, and everything to go with it, but now look at me. I ain't got shit! It just seems like I'm stuck. I'm buying bullshit dope when I'm used to grabbing a brick or better. Why? Because I ain't got money! But I'ma come back up though. Watch! Just watch. This gonna be my year!" he proclaimed.

Punkin looked into his eyes, hugged him, and kissed him on the lips.

"How much bread do you need for you to be able to get a brick thang?" she curiously asked.

"Shit, right now, I ain't got but twelve thousand to my name."

"It's gonna be alright, baby. I got just the thing to take your mind off all of your problems," she said as she undressed.

That night, the two made good love over and over again into the wee hours, which was what he needed. After hours of sex, Punkin was asleep. Uno just smiled to himself, admiring her flawless body while she slept.

***

As he cruised through the city, Uno's head was all over the place as he tried to figure out his next move. His entire world had been turned around. A drought hit the city, and the niggas who had the weight weren't selling anything over a half brick. Just Uno's luck, he only had enough money to buy a half. He could have gone to his brothers, but he wanted to show them he was his own man.

Punkin walked out to the car in a happy mood when Uno pulled into the parking lot of her workplace. When she jumped in the car, Uno just looked at her and wished he could be in a happy mood as well.

"What's up, baby? I need to go by Ace," Punkin said.

"For what?" Uno mumbled.

"Dang, I can't need something there?" Punkin asked, twisting in her seat.

Silence filled the car as the two drove to Ace. Uno's mind was in panic mode, trying to come up with a plan on how he was going to get back on his feet.

Hopping out of the car, Punkin threw extra in her hips as she walked into Ace.

Uno's cell phone started ringing as soon as Punkin shut the car door. "Hello?'

"What's up, nigga? I'm out now!" Hip Hop said.

"What's good wit' ya?" Uno asked.

Hip Hop motioned for Keisha to stop riding his dick. "Bro, you know I got that shit!" he bragged into the phone.

"Oh, yeah? And is it doing what it's supposed to do?" Uno asked.

"Yeah, nigga, and then some!" Hip Hop boasted.

Uno couldn't believe his ears. His pride was crushed because he didn't have enough bread. "What's the ticket?" he asked.

"Man, you know it's a drought in the city, so it's dried up," Hip hop stated.

"That's all fine, but I know some people who didn't get forced by the drought, and they doing pretty well with the numbers like fifteen thousand a brick," Uno stated, beating him to the punch.

Hip Hop was quiet for a minute. *'Who the fuck doing numbers like that when it's a drought in the whole Midwest?'*

Uno knew he had him when he didn't respond. "Listen, I rock with you the long way, so I'ma do twelve thousand. Just hit me up whenever you're ready to continue this relationship," Hip Hop said, motioning for Keisha to finish riding his dick.

"Yup, I'll hit ya!" Uno responded. Punkin hopped back in the car, showing all thirty-two teeth.

"What ya so happy about?" Uno asked, looking at her.

"Nothing. It's a good day." Punkin blushed.

"I can't tell it's nothing," he said, starting up the car.

"You silly, baby," she said, throwing a white envelope in his lap.

"What's this?"

"Look and see." Punkin blushed again. With suspicion in his eyes, he eyed Punkin and then opened the envelope.

His mouth dropped open while his eyes got big. Inside were crisp hundred-dollar bills. With watered eyes, he looked over at Punkin.

"Where did you get this from?" he asked

"You been all up in mines ever since I got into this car."

"Naw, I'm fo'real. Where did you get all this money from?"

"Baby, it's tax time, and I took a little out of my savings. Ain't that most of what ya need?" she asked.

"Yeah, baby." He smiled.

"Well, just know we half and half on the outcome," she teased him before letting her tongue hang out.

"Oh, yeah? Half, huh?" Uno asked, grinning from ear to ear.

"Just take your time and do whatever it is you gotta do to get back on top. I was saving up to grab me a car, but I'm coo for right now," she told him.

"Damn, baby, thank you," he said, then leaned over and gave her a wet kiss on the lips.

After the kiss, Punkin looked over at Uno, who had a new glow to himself. She grabbed his hand and interlocked it with hers.

"Uno, I want you to know I believe in you, and I will always put my last dollar on you because I know you're a very smart man. Just don't get out there and be slipping again," Punkin said, squeezing his hand.

Uno was so touched by her actions and words that he had to choke up the tears threatening to fall from his eyes. He had fire back in his eyes as he pulled out his cellphone to hit Hip Hop back. "Hip Hop, where ya be at?" he asked as soon as he picked up the phone.

Chapter 12

Uno grabbed his scale from off the table, switched it on, and started breaking down the brick into individual ounces as he pondered how he was going to maximize off the dope.

A few hours later, he had diced all the dope up and had thirty-six bags sitting around the table. He wiped down the entire kitchen with bleach as he estimated his profits. He had already made up his mind that he was gonna grind the whole brick out. He decided to change the game by selling grams for thirty dollars to lure all of the stings his way. Even with showing love, he knew he could still make at least thirty thousand if he ground everything out.

His plan was to flip the brick, grab one and a half, and keep coming back while putting money up at the same time. He still had a few loyal customers in his phone, but the little six hundred a day he was grinding up on was nothing. He knew he needed to spread his wings more on his hustle—a spot was where the money would come in.

"Yeah, that's what I need. A trap spot," Uno said as he paced around his crib. "But where at?"

***

Uno woke up early the next morning, picked up LR, and they drove around the city, hitting every hood, passing out samples with his trapline. By nightfall, they'd ground up a few thousand and gained a few new customers. They were ready to call it a night and go home when, all of a sudden, a miracle happened as they drove down Kenwood past a duplex house where he spotted the crackhead he gave his old phone to.

Uno pulled over to the house, slowly rolled down his window, and yelled, "Yo, my guy!"

The crackhead looked startled when Uno yelled for a minute, and then he hesitantly walked toward the car.

'I hope this isn't someone I owe,' the crackhead thought as he made it to Uno's car.

"This me, Uno, the one that gave you that flip phone," Uno said.

"Oh, shit!" the crackhead yelled, grabbing his dick. "Damn, man, where you been? Long time, no see," he said, kneeling to be eye level.

"I've been here and there, you know, doing my own little thang, trying to stay afloat," Uno said. "What's your name anyway?" Uno asked.

"They call me Bald-Head," he said. "Are you working?" he asked with a serious face.

"Always, baby! And it's that drop, the best in the city!" Uno boasted.

Bald-Head's face lit up. "Shit. Then, nigga, you need to pull over here and step out!"

After parking, Uno and LR followed Bald-Head inside the house, which had many different small apartments in it. The air smelled like piss and bad hygiene, but Uno and LR didn't care, because the only thing they smelled was money. The house was holding a crackhead party. Uno and LR knew they'd stumbled upon a goldmine.

"Give me a hot second. I'll be right back," Bald-Head said, then disappeared inside one of the apartments.

Looking up and down the hallway of the house, Uno shook his head. Trash, dust, bottles, and blotches filled the hallway. Counting the rooms, Uno rubbed his hands together, knowing money was going to pour in like clockwork. He scanned the house again to look for an escape route because he didn't plan to get caught slipping again. The whole time they stood in the hallway, crackheads walked back and forth like The Walking Dead, working their brains, trying to figure out where they were going to get their next hit.

Bald-Head came out of the apartment with a Kool-Aid smile and handed Uno a hundred dollars.

"Look out for me, too!" Bald-Head said.

Uno gave LR a nod, and he pulled out three fat grams and dropped them in Bald-Head's hand. Bald-Head's eyes light up like a Christmas tree. He looked like he had just found out he'd gotten a million dollars. He looked down at his hand in disbelief because he hadn't seen rocks this big since Big Dawg and Ant had spots in his hood, Hard Part.

"Damn, y'all holding like this?"

"Every day! And I'm doing grams for thirty to forty!" Uno bragged, feeling better.

"I'll be back in a minute!" he said, walking back into the same apartment.

For the remainder of the day, all Bald-Head did was come in and out of apartments with wads of cash. By nighttime, Uno had rushed back home many times to grab more dope.

"Man, y'all need to stop bullshitting and grab one of these apartments in here!" Bald-Head said, looking at Uno and LR count wads of cash.

Uno stopped counting and looked at Bald-Head and asked, "They got some apartments open?"

"Yeah, five or six are open!"

Uno put the money inside his pocket. "Why you didn't tell us this a while ago? And don't nobody be tryna open shop over here?" Uno asked.

"I wasn't thinking, and a couple of them young dudes be coming through, but with that dope y'all got, and me working these apartments, we can lock this shit down!" Bald-Head replied.

"Who do we need to holla at to grab some rooms?" LR smirked.

Bald-Head smiled back. "Follow me," he said and led them to the owner's room. When Bald-Head knocked on the door, a short, old, fat man answered.

"My nephews here new in town and wanna get a room," Bald-Head said, looking at Uno and LR, smiling.

"Come in," the old man said, looking them up and down.

When they entered the apartment, an odor slapped them in the face. The smell was so bad that both Uno and LR almost threw up in their mouths. The apartment was so hot it felt like he had ten ovens on. The owner had two crackhead females sitting around. The old man grabbed a set of keys off the table before walking Uno, LR, and Bald-Head toward one of the available apartments.

The owner stopped in front of apartment six and opened the door, where the place was disorganized. The walls were stained with yellow stuff, the carpet was white but looked black and brown in different places, flies were everywhere, and the roaches patrolled the whole floor.

"It needs a little work to it," the owner said, fanning flies out of the way.

"Take us to see the other room," Uno said. The owner walked to the apartment next door, which was in a little better condition.

"If you don't mind me asking, what's a few big fellas like y'all selves wanting with an apartment in this shit hole?" the owner asked.

"I'ma gonna be honest with you, old school. We tryna grind out of here," Uno replied.

"That's okay with me as long as you keep them young boys out of here with that loud cussing and music," the owner said, nodding his head.

"Now I don't even get down with them youngsters. This is my brother and the only one you will see," Uno said, pointing at LR.

"Well, I know Bald-Head here will let you know that I get down with the get down and like to drink sometimes," the owner said.

"What you tryna do?" Uno asked LR.

"Let's do us, bro," LR said with a smile on his face, knowing they were about to get money.

Uno smiled, then handed the owner three grams and five hundred dollars. "Is that coo with you?" Uno asked.

"Hell yeah. This looks like we're gonna have a beautiful relationship," the owner said. "Let me explain a few things to you and you for a minute. The rent is a hundred dollars a week, and I'll need two weeks' rent upfront, which we already have covered. I usually lock the front door at ten o'clock during the weekdays and eleven o'clock on the weekends, but as long as you take care of me, I will take care of you and waive the rules. Now, which room are you picking?"

"We want both of them," LR said.

Uno peeled off another hundred, handing it to the old man, who had a surprised look on his face as he handed the keys to both apartments to Uno. He reached his hand out for a shake, but Uno dapped him, followed by LR.

"Nice meeting you," Uno said, then headed to the first apartment.

Bald-Head was right behind them. "Why y'all grab two rooms?" he asked.

Uno looked at LR for an answer, too.

"Because I'm going to chill in one, and the other, we going to make into a smoking galleria, and the crackheads can take tricks there for only five dollars an hour."

"Damn, lil' bro. That was a smart move," Uno said to LR.

After they found a stash spot, Uno and LR stashed their dope and locked up so the three could go to CVS on 38th for some cleaning supplies and other things to go around the spot.

Later that night, Uno paid the two crackheads inside the owner's spot to clean both apartments thoroughly. Then he placed roach bombs in each corner and called it a night.

***

Uno drove around to Ashley's spot to see if Nasty was free to hang out. The two grabbed a bottle of VSOP then cruised around the city, smoking, catching up on each other's lives. Having the heart-to-heart got both of them emotional when they started talking about Nasty's cousin Juan, and before they knew it, Uno was pulling up to the graveyard. The night fog had the graveyard looking scarier than it was.

"Come on, nigga. Let's go pay our respects," Uno said, walking toward Juan's gravesite. Nasty wasn't at all scared, but why the hell did they have to pay their respects at night? They could have pulled up when it was daytime.

"Your lil' cousin with me," Uno said, walking all the way up to Juan's tombstone as he sipped from his bottle.

For the next few minutes, the two stood in front of Juan's tombstone and paid their respects. Twenty minutes later, they were parked in front of Ashley's crib. Uno hollered at Nasty about the plan to get back on his feet with the two apartments he and LR had and let him know he could come in with him.

When Nasty dropped his head, he already knew what time it was because he had the same look when Punkin was talking to him.

Basically, Nasty was tired of Uno always having to help him out. He gave Uno love, hopped out, and walked to the front door. Uno waited to see if he made it in safely, blew the horn, and pulled off.

Chapter 13

When Uno and LR arrived back at the spot the next morning, there were roaches, ants, and rats dead all through the house. The two stood at the door, staring inside the apartment as both shook their heads.

"We got a lot of work to do," he said to LR.

Uno immediately had Bald-Head go around and recruited a few crackheads to clean and remodel both apartments to look like somewhere someone could stay. Uno was determined to get back on top, so he confined himself to the trap, only leaving to take a shower or to take Punkin to work and pick her back up.

Whenever the trap wasn't booming, Uno and LR would walk around, handing out samples to recruit new customers and letting them know they had a spot on Kenwood.

Within a few weeks, all you heard were Uno's and LR's names in every crackheads mouth. Money started pouring in once word got on the street about them having grams for thirty to forty dollars. They weren't seeing anything less than eight thousand a day and ten thousand on the weekends. Business was good for them. Then he went out and dropped fifteen thousand on a used Lexus for Punkin. Not only had he given Punkin her money back, but he had given her double.

Besides paying bills, buying clothes and shoes, he saved every penny they made. They were grinding hard. He started to be strict with himself and LR so they would never have to ask for any help from anyone. Uno had that hunger in him again to the point he'd seen the light at the end, and he was just getting started.

Chapter 14

Uno's Gucci loafers and Punkin's three-hundred-dollar Chanel heels hit the hard floor, sounding like they were making a beat as the couple made their way toward the courtroom to see what lay ahead for Uno's fate. Punkin squeezed Uno's hand to let him know she was there and had his back no matter what.

When Uno's case was called an hour late. Hennessy had the judge dismissed since their key witnesses had been killed in a hotel with the undercover cop in Anderson.

Uno turned toward Hennessy, who gratefully shook her hand, thanked her for her services, and told her that she was his new lawyer now.

***

For a few months, Uno's and LR's business had been booming. Uno had a spot, and LR had one in their hood, but both spots really ran themselves. Growing up, watching Big Dawg and them, they knew they had to treat their spots like it was a Fortune 500 business. They were players, and they helped out crackheads who were sick by giving them dope. They even threw block parties for all to come. They gave out prizes to people who won games—kids, grown-ups, crackheads—whoever was welcome to come.

The time Uno and LR spent grinding, they never knew different crews were feeling the effect, and they were making enemies along the way to the top. Man-Man's crew was also becoming envious that all his clientele was going Uno's and LR's way.

Two-Tall and Tru drove by Uno's spot on 29th MLK to peep out how they were running their trap. When they pulled up on the block, they saw a lot of their regulars standing around with Kool-Aid smiles on their faces. This had their blood boiling. They parked their car a few houses down and sat while monitoring the traffic.

Twenty minutes later, Two-Tall decided it was enough. Watching the traffic go in and out of Uno's spot had him fuming because their money flow had slowed down. Bald-Head and Two-Tall made eye contact as Bald-Head drove his bike past their car. He alerted Uno and LR that a black Toyota with tints was a few houses down, watching their spot.

Standing in the front yard, Uno and LR mugged the car with hands full of money. As the car slowly pulled off, Two-Tall mugged the two back.

"We gonna have a problem wit' them two," Two-Tall told Tru as they made their way back to their own spot on 25th Street.

More and more clientele paired into both of their spots as the weeks passed by. Uno and LR were grinding so hard they could barely get any rest. With each passing day, they accumulated something new. If it weren't clothes, DVDs, TVs, house supplies, jewelry, games, free food cards, it was pictures of tricks having parties with judges, lawyers, and/or police officers.

Things went to the next level when LR recruited his cousin Mo-Mo, and he opened a candy-food store in one of the apartments. By now, they had six apartments working for them.

Uno saw money from all angles. If he could put a dollar down and see two come back, he would be good. Bald-Head hung around Uno so much that he became his eyes, ears, and right hand.

Uno would chill out in his apartment, while Bald-Head handled all the transactions. The few girls he recruited tricked out of one apartment. New faces were popping up as word traveled about Uno's and LR's spot shop, where you could get your dick sucked, get food, and smoke. Whenever someone popped up, they didn't know Bald-Head would make them hit the pipe in front of him to make sure they weren't getting set up by the police.

Uno didn't play when it came to his spot. That was his money maker, so if it wasn't about buying dope, tricking with one of the girls, or buying food from the store, you had to go because he didn't let anyone loiter in the hallways.

In a matter of months, Uno and LR were copping over ten bricks. Instead of just breaking them all down, he made LR sell weight while Bald-Head sold nickels and dimes from the other spot. He made sure never to put cut on his dope, so he sold it as-was.

The non-stop grinding started to take its toll on Uno's and LR's bodies. Sometimes, they would let Nasty or Mo-Mo run their spots, but Nasty was always on a pussy hunt, and Mo-Mo only wanted to get high off Stick's wet. That meant the spot would be left open for whoever to come and get their money, and Uno didn't play that, because they put too much sweat, time, and grind into building their spots, so, instead of letting them run the spot, Uno would hit Nasty with his own work. That way, he could grind how he wanted, and LR would do the same with Mo-Mo.

Uno had his eye on another candidate named Lil' E, whom he really took a liking to. He was different than the rest of the hustlers he sold work to out there. All those hustlers out there, and all they did was smoke, drink, mess with females, and stunt like they were getting money, whereas Lil' E was out on the block, grinding, stacking his bread. He didn't drink, smoke, or do any other shit.

For the past month, he watched Lil' E turn a quad into a whole brick, which was impressive to Uno. Lil' E stayed a few houses down with his auntie and lil' cousin. When Uno looked into Lil' E's eyes, he saw hunger and determination, so one day, he pulled up on him and gave him the opportunity to work in the apartment at night. When Lil' E heard what Uno was talking about, he jumped on it without thinking. Who wouldn't? Uno's spot was one of, if not the most, booming spots on the west side.

Lil' E went out east to a family member's house, and they were talking about Uno's and LR one-shop spot.

Uno sat in the spot with Lil' E for a few weeks, breaking shit down to him and seeing how he handled his business. After Uno thought Lil' E was ready to stand on his own ten, he let him do him. With someone who knew how to handle business, Uno fell back to let his body rest a little.

Meanwhile, Punkin was on her grind as well, working full-time every day while going to night school. She already had her future mapped out because that was where she would be. No matter their schedules, Punkin and Uno always found time to have family time. Supporting each other, they worked together to make it happen. Actually, with them not spending a lot of time with each other, when they did have sex, it was more stimulating.

Although Uno wasn't spending money on himself, he always gave Punkin and their daughter gifts and kept Punkin's hair and nails done. Every time Uno flipped a package, he accumulated more and more wealth. Before he knew it, the summer was hitting again. His money had piled up, and after taking a few losses, he still managed to stack over $170,000. That was only the beginning for him.

Chapter 15

Uno was awakened by the sounds of gunshots ringing throughout the neighborhood. Sitting up, he yawned and wiped the sleep from his eyes. The spot was booming so hard last night that he didn't make it home. He had only been asleep for a few hours.

That day was Punkin's graduation. She would be walking across the stage to get her GED, and he was so proud of her. She had ambition, and he loved that about her.

When he was locked up, she was the one who motivated him to continue with his GED. He was thinking about going to night school to get his degree. He didn't plan to stay in the streets long; the game was a stepping stone for him. Risks had to be taken to get ahead.

Hennessy had gamed him on this financial advisor, who was one of the best in the business, so he had seen numbers like fifteen to twenty percent returns.

Uno looked at his phone. It was nine in the morning, and Lil' E was due to pull up so he could relieve him. He hopped up and went to get his hygiene together so he could start his long day. While he was washing his face, he heard a knock at the door.

"What it do, fam?" Uno asked Bald-Head.

"Same shit, different day," Bald-Head said, walking all the way into the apartment. "Here," he said, handing him a wad of cash.

Uno went over and grabbed his sock. "Here you go," he said, throwing Bald-Head a little extra something.

"Good looking out, bro!" Bald-Head said and disappeared back out the door.

***

Uno headed into the Gucci store to grab his clothes.

"Hello, Uno!" two girls said in unison when he walked through the door.

Uno smiled. "Damn, I don't know if I came to get my clothes or to see them beautiful smiles on y'all faces," he flirted, walking up to the counter.

Both girls just giggled.

After he paid his six-hundred-dollar bill, one of the girls helped him carry his bags out to his car.

Uno stared across the street and saw the same car he had seen the day Bald-Head said they were watching his spot. Smiling, Uno acknowledged to the car that he knew they were following him.

"Yeah, nigga, I see ya bitch ass," Two-Tall said as he puffed on a blunt.

Uno was fucking with their pockets, so in return, he planned on fucking up his.

When Uno pulled into the parking lot, it was packed. Arriving at the auditorium, he scanned the crowd. Mrs. Brew saw Uno looking for them, so she stood up and waved him over to their section.

Smoothly, Uno walked over to where Punkin's family awaited. He walked down the aisle, looking like he just popped out of GQ magazine, leaving the scent of his high-priced Gucci cologne lingering in the air. After saying hello, he went and took his seat by Punkin's mother and LR.

As the graduates walked into the auditorium, Punkin's entire family stood and yelled her name, making her blush hard.

Punkin looked at Uno and blew him a kiss and mouthed the words, *I love you.*

He nodded his head and said it in return.

The master of ceremonies began his speech after the graduating class took their seats. By the time the master of ceremonies finished his speech, he had everyone on their feet, giving him a standing ovation. The moment had finally come, which everyone had been waiting for.

The dean called Punkin's name about ten minutes after he began, and her family stood and cheered like they were at the game. Everyone took their pictures as Punkin, holding her diploma up for all to see, stood in front of the auditorium.

After the graduation, Uno treated the whole family to eat out. Thanks to Uno's connections, the entire twenty were able to get a seat within minutes of arriving. They exchanged casual talk while they waited for their food to arrive. Uno made sure he ordered bottles of champagne to go with their food, water for those who didn't drink, and juice or pop for the kids.

He stood up and tapped his glass, causing everyone in the room to grow quiet. Everyone's eyes got big when Uno reached into his suit jacket pocket and pulled out a Tiffany's box. Some of Punkin's family's mouths were open, while others had their hands holding their chests. She looked around at her family, who, in return, were anxiously waiting for her to open it.

"Okay. Okay. Here I go," Punkin said, finally opening it.

"Oh my God!" everyone yelled.

Punkin sat with her mouth open. Inside was a six-karat diamond platinum ring.

"This is a graduation present, baby, and here," he said, handing her a paper while smiling.

"Baby, I love the ring," Punkin said, setting the paper down and handing Uno the ring to put on her finger. "What's this paper?" she asked, opening it up.

"It's a little something," he said, sitting down.

"What is it, sis?" LR asked, wanting to know.

"It's a bank account for me and Pooder with a hundred thousand on it and a deed to a house," he told him.

"Where you getting all this money from at the age you are?" Punkin's auntie asked with her nose up.

"Why?" Punkin's mom asked, not liking that she would ask that type of question.

For the next hour, everyone had fun, sitting there, stuffing their faces, and enjoying their time.

Uno picked up the tub while everyone gave out hugs and kisses in the parking lot. Punkin hopped in the car with Uno. She yelled, "Bye," as they were pulling off.

Chapter 16

Everyone's block that Uno drove past had a firework stand. With it being July 4th, Uno was planning to take Punkin and his daughter to see the fireworks downtown. He was trying to get her to go off to college somewhere nearby, but she was fighting him on it, saying she didn't want to leave him, her family, and friends. He was so proud of her anyway.

Nasty was impatiently waiting for Uno when he pulled up on Edgemont in a Lexus truck. He hopped in, and Uno served him, and then Uno headed to Man's Fashion to grab a fit for the night.

By six o'clock, Uno was heading to the crib to get ready. Having not seen Punkin all day, he decided to call her.

"Hello?" Punkin answered unhappily.

"What's wrong with you?" Uno asked, concerned.

"Nothing. It's just… don't worry about it, baby," Punkin said with a hint of frustration as she comforted her mother while she cried.

"Who's crying? Listen. I can hear it in your voice that something ain't right. I'm right around the corner. I'll be there in a hot second," Uno said and hung up.

When Punkin opened the door, looking like she had lost her dog, Uno immediately knew something was wrong.

"Baby, what's wrong?" Uno asked, stepping inside the house. "Talk to me." He lifted her chin to meet his eyes.

Looking around the house, he saw Mrs. Brew off in the corner, sitting on the sofa, crying. Her face and nose were red, and by the looks of it, she'd been crying all day.

"What's going on? Can one of you please talk to me?" Uno asked with a grimace.

"Today, we were hit with bad news," Punkin said. Mrs. Brew started crying again, and Punkin went to comfort her while Pooder walked over to Uno.

"What's the bad news?" Uno asked with concern in his voice.

"Today, Momma's job had to let her go because the company been downsizing, and she been crying because she don't know how she going to finish paying the house off."

Uno sat down on the edge of the sofa and shook his head, sympathetically looking at the pair. "How much?"

"She'll be alright," Punkin said as she hugged her mother.

"How much?" Uno asked again while walking up to the two.

"Forty thousand," Mrs. Brew said, looking up in his sincere eyes.

"I'll be back." Uno nodded, setting Pooder down.

"Don't go out and do nothing silly, baby," Punkin said, blocking his path.

"Baby, she has to have a place she can call hers, so I'm goin' to stop at the spot me & LR have. I'll be back through around seven or eight to pick y'all back up for the fireworks. Goodbye, Mrs. Brew." He waved and then left through the front door.

**

A man of his word, Uno was standing on Punkin's momma's porch at eight. Punkin answered the door, looking gorgeous, holding Pooder in her arms.

"We ready?" She walked onto the front porch.

"Coo, hold on. Let me go holler at your mom right fast. I will be out in a minute," he said, disappearing inside the house, holding a bag in his hand.

Punkin just shook her head with a smile because it touched her heart that he really cared for her and her family.

Uno walked into Mrs. Brew's room and handed her the bag. "Mrs. Brew, I need you to hold this for me for a while."

"What is it, baby?"

"The money for the house and a little extra for you," Uno said with a smirk.

Mrs. Brew opened the bag and had almost had a heart attack. "Oh, God!" she screamed. "Uno, I—I can't. She shook her head with tears pouring down her face.

Uno just shook his head when she tried to hand him the bag back.

"You can, and you will. That came from both me and your son," he said.

Punkin ran back into the house to grab Pooder's bottle when she stopped to see what Uno and her mother were talking about. Uno never ceased to amaze her every time she turned around.

Uno walked over to Mrs. Brew and gave her a kiss.

"Thank you, baby!"

"It's fifty thousand. The extra is to help with whatever," he said. Mrs. Brew was about to say something, but Uno stopped her by saying," Goodnight, Mrs. Brew." Then he waved as he walked out of her room.

"Bye, Mom," Punkin said.

***

When Uno arrived downtown, it was packed. Cars were bumper to bumper. He drove around for the next fifteen minutes, looking for a parking space. After finding a nice parking spot, the two walked while Uno pushed the stroller to the gathering. The fireworks were just starting. Different colors illuminated the night sky. Pooder clapped her small hands as she watched.

"I got a surprise for you, baby," he whispered in her ear.

"What is it?" she spun around and asked with a big smile on her face.

"I'm gonna send you, Petra, and Patricia to the spa," he said.

"You know, you are something else," Punkin said, shaking her head and staring at him with amazement in her eyes.

"I got you, baby," he told her with a smile.

After the fireworks ended, they drove to BW3 and ordered some wings, fries, and chocolate chip cookies.

Even though they were young, it seemed that they were older. They looked so perfect together that a few couples in the place thought they were newlyweds. After finishing their food, they took a little stroll. Pooder was sound asleep.

"It look so beautiful out here," Punkin said.

"Yeah, it does, don't it?" Uno replied, looking up at the black sky. He and Punkin were staring at two different things. In Uno's eyes, he saw a city he planned to take over one day.

"Baby, how long do you plan on being in the streets? Because every person we know either dead or in jail," she said.

He stopped walking and spun her around so they could be eye to eye.

"Listen. I been thinking about starting a crew to where we can get this money faster because I have a plan to be out the streets in the next two years. By that time, me, you, and Pooder can move into a nice crib…"

"But—" Punkin attempted.

"Listen!" Uno cut her off. "Baby, a lot of sacrifices are gonna have to be made on both of our ends. With you standing next to me, we can have the world. We have to be strong."

Punkin nodded that she understood what he was talking about, but then dropped her head. All her thoughts were of Uno getting gunned down or thrown back in jail.

"There's no woman in this whole world that can take my heart from you. When we old enough, we gonna get married," Uno said, lifting her chin. "Right now, I need you to only focus on school and our daughter, and I got the rest. Can you do that for me?" he asked.

Punkin nodded her head as she looked into his eyes.

"That's my girl," he said, kissing her cheek as they headed to the car.

"One thing, though," Punkin said when they got to the car.

"What?" he asked.

"When you do feel like it's time to ask me to marry you, I don't want a ring. Buy me a apartment building because marriage is about growth, and we can't grow off no ring."

Chapter 17

Nasty toured the streets in disbelief at how bad his luck was. He couldn't figure out why it was so hard for him to come up and stay up. Not only was he behind on rent, but he also needed a car. The sting he used to leave dope with had been knocked the other night, and Ashley was due in a few months.

As Nasty drove down Roach's block, smoking on a blunt, he thought about how Ashley had been acting funny toward him. He didn't understand how a female could sleep next to a nigga and not give him any pussy or head but then turn around and ask him to pay a bill.

Since Nasty was out west, he decided to swing by Uno's spot and see if he was back from out of town. Traffic was booming when he pulled up, just as expected.

"What's good, Nasty? I think the nigga in there sleep," Bald-Head told him as he walked the hallway with rocks in his hand.

Nasty knocked on the door.

"Who dat be?" Uno asked.

"Damn, nigga, it's the one and only!"

Uno unlocked and opened the door. "Damn, bro, what brings you over my way?" he asked as Nasty walked in.

"I'm stressing hard, bro!" he replied, taking a seat in the recliner. "Nigga, you look tired as hell!"

Uno rubbed his eyes and nodded his head. After Nasty shared his misfortunes, Uno replied, "Shit, why don't you post up and get your bread straight?"

"Naw, bro, you gotta stop trying to help me out. You doing your thing over here. I gotta stand up and be a man and stop depending on you."

"Nigga, you tripping hard! If I got it, you got it!"

"What I need is a nice lick," Nasty said, sparking up a blunt.

Uno sat back in his chair and looked over at Nasty. He could see the look of hunger and desperation written all over Nasty's face. Even though he had two spots, his cash wasn't at all like people thought, so he would ride or die with his nigga on anything he wanted.

"You know who I seen at Mrs. Kim's store the other day?" he asked Uno.

"Who?"

"Man-Man. How the fuck that nigga get on like that? If memory serves me right, wasn't he one of them safe, spoiled niggas when we were growing up? I'm telling you, Uno, soft ass niggas like him don't deserve to be at the top of the game!" Nasty said, shaking his head. "And then the nigga gonna look at me with a smirk on his face and flash a bankroll like he knows I'm on the floor."

Uno laughed. "When I came home, the nigga drove down mom's block and shot me a few bucks. Then he had the nerve to shoot me his number and told me to holla at him if I needed a job, but the thing is, he was fuckin' with Punkin when we were locked up, and when she didn't give him the pussy, he played her, I guess," Uno said.

"Who the fuck this nigga think he is?" Nasty hopped up and asked.

"That's the nigga I'm goin' to touch," he said, rubbing his chin and looking at Uno.

"The nigga ya going to touch, huh? I thought we were a family?" Uno asked.

Nasty smirked, too. "So you down, bro?"

"Yeah, I'm down. You bro, and plus, it's really time to turn up!" Uno said, standing up.

"I been thinking about putting a crew together so we can take over more of the hood, feel me? Because right now, it's only me, LR, Lil' E, Mo-Mo, and you if you down."

"Hell yeah!" Nasty said, smiling. Man-Man had been around the city, stunting extra hard, showcasing his new jewelry, touring in his Jaguar truck. Word on the streets was his cousin cut him off, and he linked up with an old school named Red that was moving major weight. The thing was, no one knew how to get at Man-Man, because he kept his inner circle small. It was like he would make his money and disappear when no one was looking. Uno picked many brains, trying to figure it out. One chick from their hood pulled down and gave him the 4-1-1.

Man-Man had been messing with a chick named Tee, but somewhere, things went bad with their relationship. There was nothing like a scarred woman. Tee's name rang in Uno's head.

'Tee? Tee? Tee? Damn, I remember I went to school with a Tee, with her little ass,' Uno thought. He already had the info on where he could find Tee, and he knew what he had to do. He pulled his cell phone out and dialed Nasty's number, who picked right up.

"What's up, nigga?"

"Yo, I'ma need you to pull up on me later on," Uno said.

"Aight, I'll be through there. I hope you got some good news for a nigga too. Shit looking ugly. I'm about to pull a solo dolo lick to hold me over," Nasty said.

"Just chill out, nigga. I got you!" Uno laughed.

Nasty had a few hours left before he had to meet up with Uno. He fired up a blunt and sipped on his bottle. As the tunes of Boosie blasted through the speakers, he thought about how tired he was of small dogging the sack. Times like that made him feel some type of way. Out of all the years he'd been touching a sack, he never had over twenty range on his own.

Life had dealt him a fucked-up hand. Besides, the fact that he never really fucked with his father, his mother had to work extra hard to put shoes, clothes, and food on the table to the point that Nasty turned toward the streets. The streets were all he knew. He'd been in the streets as long as he could remember, and just like Uno, Big Dawg and Ant had taught him the ropes of the game.

Nasty felt like the streets owed him something, so he walked around with a chip on his shoulder. He knew the niggas that were on top didn't have half the heart he did, so why did they get to ball?

**

Nasty, LR, and Baby J were parked in front of the spot when Uno pulled up. He hopped out of the car and ran into the spot. The minute he opened the door, he saw Lil' E cuddled on the sofa with a female that Uno had seen somewhere before.

Before Uno could say anything, the female rushed into the bathroom. Knowing that Uno never handled transactions in front of anyone, Lil' E was glad she remembered to excuse herself. Uno handed Lil' E his work once he saw the female was gone. He made a mental to check him when he pulled back up to the spot.

Nasty was on his cell when Uno hopped in the rental. By the way the call was going, he must've been on the phone with Ashley. Uno looked at him, then at LR and Baby J, shaking his head. Nasty was catching heat from all ends of the stick, so Uno knew this lick was a must for him.

Nasty shook his head when he hung up the phone.

"What's good with you?" he asked, giving Uno dap.

"Man, sometimes the bitch Ashley be getting in my head to the point I want to put two in her head! Tell me, you got some good news for me."

"Nigga, swing by the L right fast." Uno laughed. After grabbing their bottles, the four toured around the whole city as Uno filled them in on all the information he had received about Man-Man's ex-girlfriend, Tee.

Nasty smiled. He already knew what Uno was thinking, but he decided to joke with him anyway.

"Nigga, if it's the same Tee we went to Washington with, how you know she gonna remember you?"

"Nigga, a female never forgets Uno! Once I got you, I'm in your life for good!" he arrogantly joked.

"While you thinking you a player, you better be worried about my sister, nigga," LR said.

"That's real life, lil' cuz. Punkin really not goin' to let you be out here throwing your dick around, so ya better be careful, and you not no playa. You just watch too many movies," Baby J said, laughing.

All four men laughed as Nasty pulled into the gas station on 29th and MLK.

"Look at this nigga," Nasty said as he tapped Uno and pointed at Man-Man.

Man-Man and his crew cruised around the parking lot as they stared at them. Word had gotten back to Uno that Man-Man was getting fronted his bricks, and that could've been true. Man-Man had a crew behind him.

As Nasty cruised around the parking lot, Uno locked eyes with Black Tone. It was crazy how money could make a nigga cocky. Itis ass was leaning up against his black Beamer with his shirt wide open, showing off his chest like he was some sort of sex symbol.

"Bitch ass muthafucka," Uno mumbled. After spending a few minutes parking lot pimping, Nasty dropped them back off at Uno's spot, with them all agreeing to meet up at Jacqueline's Soul Food for lunch the next day. Uno immediately grew upset when he walked into the spot and found Lil' E sitting at the table, talking to a stranger.

Lil' E stood up and immediately intervened.

"This is my cousin Babyface, who just came home from jail. He straight," he said.

Uno furiously gritted his teeth. He looked Babyface up and down with a grimace on his face and pulled out his Glock.

"I don't know this nigga! If you don't get this nigga out of my spot, I'ma start busting in this muthafucka," he said, cocking the Glock to show he meant business.

"Aight, I'ma going to be outside, lil' cuz," Babyface said, biting down on his tongue, walking toward the door, but before he walked out, he turned and looked at Uno in his eyes and said, "Listen. I respect your gangsta, but that gun don't scare niggas like myself, but since this your spot, I'm goin' to head out, but all I'm trying to do is get money, so if I have to, I will show you what I can bring to the table. I'm gonna let that soak in your head," Babyface said, walking out.

"Nigga, what the fuck is wrong wit' you?" Uno asked.

"I-I-I—" Lil' E stuttered.

"Listen here, lil' nigga. As long as I'm living, I don't ever wanna walk in this spot again and see another muthafucka sitting up in my shit! You hear me?" Uno yelled.

Lil' E nodded. If Uno had been anyone else, he would have shot that nigga for talking to him like that, but he knew Uno looked at him like a little brother and only wanted the best for him, so he took it.

"That goes for hoes, homeboys, anybody! This is a business, not a damn hangout spot." Uno continued to talk as he moved around the house. "The last thing we need is someone watching our pockets! I put too much work into building this shit from the ground up, and I'll be damned if I let a nigga like you fuck it up. Next thing you know, niggas will be tryna short stop our bread!" Uno preached to him.

"My bad, bro," Lil' E said, realizing Uno was absolutely right. He put trust in him when no one would, and he took that for granted. He was slipping, and this was a man's game where slipping could cost you your life. This was all he had.

"Where's that bread at?" Uno asked. "Tighten up your shit, nigga. I got something in the works that's going to put us on top," he said and left.

As soon as Uno hopped inside the rental, he grabbed the blunt out of the ashtray and lit it. It was 2:30 a.m. His body and mind were exhausted, and he had a bad headache. To relax, he slipped in the slow jams mix Punkin made for him, heading to the crib for the night.

***

Uno and LR were parked in front of the restaurant where Tee worked, patiently waiting for her to come out. Thirty minutes later, Tee exited the restaurant. LR hit Uno's arm, and he attentively sat up in his seat.

"Damn, Tee done got bad!" he said.

"Hell yeah," LR said, watching her ass move left to right.

Drool dropped from their mouths as they watched Tee sashay down the sidewalk. She still had that peanut buttercup skin that made her look like she was from India or something. Uno couldn't get over how bad and thick Tee had gotten. Lil' Tomboy Tee had transformed into a five-five, 140-pound goddess. Niggas and bitches were turning around to admire her backside as she passed them.

"I be back, bro," Uno said, hopping out of the car as soon as she disappeared into another restaurant. When Uno walked in, Tee was standing at the counter, placing her order. He shook his head, admiring Tee from the back. *'Damn, I need to hit that,'* he said to himself.

Tee paid for her order, and when she spun around, she covered her mouth with one hand. "Oh, shit! Uno!"

Uno played it off like he didn't know who she was. He squinted his eyes, walked closer, and asked, "Tee?"

With a gigantic smile, Tee nodded her head.

"Oh, shit!" Uno said as he swaggered toward her, and the two embraced for the first time in years.

Tee was in shock. She stepped back and looked at him from head to toe. "Oh, my God. You look good! Look at you," she said, looking at Uno wearing Louis Vuitton with a pair of Men's solid acetate Aviator sunglasses that she knew cost a few hundred. She shook her head. "You done got all buffed up," she said, playfully punching him in the arm.

"Next, please!" the cashier yelled, interrupting the reunion.

"Hold up, Tee. Let me order my food real quick." While Uno placed his order, Tee admired his new physique.

'Damn, this nigga looking good as shit. I wouldn't mind his ass throwing me in the air and fuckin' the shit out of this pussy. I bet he must be getting money, by the looks of it,' she thought to herself.

Uno caught Tee in the act when he spun around. "So, you like what you see?" he asked, smiling.

"Yes, I like what I see. Do you?" she asked.

Uno laughed. "Yeah, I like what I see, even when you was a tomboy."

Tee playfully punched him in the arm again. "You always was tight with your tongue," she replied, staring deeply into his eyes.

"Damn. Ms. Tee, or is it Mrs.?" Uno asked.

"It's still Miss," she said, smiling.

"Man, last I heard, your mom moved y'all to LA," Uno said.

"We did for a minute, but my momma got bored out that way. She was doing some modeling but got homesick, so she moved us back since we was back and forth in the first place. She still doing her thing, but right now, she just opened that restaurant down the street."

Uno nodded his head.

"So, who's the lucky lady you have?" she asked Uno, fishing for information.

Uno smiled. "Right now, me and Punkin still doin' our thing, and we just had a baby girl."

Tee rolled her eyes.

"What about yourself?" he asked.

"Well, I just got out of a bad relationship, and after what that nigga pulled, we definitely won't be getting back together. I caught his ass in my bed, cheating with this rat bitch! I mean, if you're gonna cheat, at least cheat with a bad bitch. Don't downgrade," she said, shaking her head.

"Your orders are ready!" the cashier told the two.

Tee checked her watch. "Oh, shit! I've been over here twenty minutes. I'm supposed to be making these orders." She grabbed Uno's phone and put her number in it. "Call me!" she said, kissed him on the cheek, and charged out the door.

Uno grabbed a few condiments and headed out to the car.

"Phase one of our plan has been completed. Now, it's time to move on to the next," Uno said to LR.

Chapter 18

"This the dress to wear, girl. I'm telling you," Tee's cousin September said while holding up a dress that would show off every curve Tee had.

"Alright, damn," Tee responded, slipping into the dress. That night, Tee wanted everything to be perfect. Everything from her purse and her outfit to her perfume had to be right. After a week of phone tag, Uno had finally asked her out on a date. Tee desperately needed to get out and have a good time, and that night, she planned on doing just that. After seeing how fine Uno had gotten over the years, he had her hormones in overdrive even though he said he and Punkin were still doing their thing. She didn't know what Uno had planned for them, but she knew she had pussy for him.

Meanwhile, Uno was stepping out of the shower. He dried off, headed to his bedroom, and looked at the clock on the wall.

'It's only eight o'clock. I got two hours,' he said to himself, standing in his walk-in closet, searching for the perfect outfit for the night.

Image was everything to him. The bigger his bankroll got, the sicker his dress game upgraded. Since it was a breezy night, he decided to wear a pair of brown Burberry slacks, a Burberry silk shirt, and a pair of Burberry loafers. He grabbed a pair of matching silk boxers, got dressed, then squirted on some Burberry cologne and bounced out the door.

After making a few rounds, Uno pulled up to Tee's house around 9:50 p.m.

"Girl, he's here!" September announced as she peeped through the curtains, seeing him pull up.

"How do I look, girl?" Tee asked nervously.

September nodded her head, pointed at her, and said, "You killing that dress!"

When the doorbell rang, Tee took a deep breath and opened the door. Looking at Uno standing on her porch had her speechless.

'Damn, this nigga looks better and better every time I see him.'

"You ready to go?" Uno asked with a smile.

"Yes," Tee said, walking onto the porch and shutting the door.

September just shook her head and smiled. *'Damn that nigga is cold,'* she thought.

"So, do I look okay?" Tee asked, doing a 360-degree spin for him.

Uno nodded his head.

Tee was wearing a sexy, black Alexander McQueen dress with spaghetti straps with a matching clutch purse. She was displaying her fresh French pedicure in a pair of open-toed heels and was wearing a fragrance that made Uno's dick jump in his pants.

"Alright, don't wait up for me," Tee said loud enough for September to hear through the open window.

During the entire ride to BW3's, Uno and Tee joked and giggled while catching up on each other's lives. The more Uno put a smile on Tee's face she eyed him with more of a grin.

After finally finding a parking space, he parked and then walked over to the passenger side to help Tee out of the car like the perfect gentleman he was. Inside, the lobby was packed with couples waiting to be seated.

"Damn, we gonna be here forever." She pouted.

"Give me a hot second," Uno said, excusing himself.

After walking over and whispering a few words in the hostess's ear, she nodded, grabbed two menus, and escorted them to a table in the back.

Tee couldn't do anything but shake her head as they both followed behind the hostess. *'This nigga is something,'* she thought.

Uno waited for Tee to place her order first, when the waitress came to their table, like a gentleman. She ordered a shrimp tail platter with a Caesar salad, and Uno ordered the wing platter with a Caesar salad also.

When their orders arrived, they were enjoying themselves. The more they sipped their drinks, the more they cracked jokes on people sitting around them. Tee was really having fun. Uno just patiently sat back and watched her down her second drink. Then he smiled to himself because he knew it was about that time to pick her brain.

"So, Ms. Tee, what's ol' dudes name who you was dealing with?" Uno asked.

"Who? Man-Man?" she asked, rolling her eyes.

"Man-Man? That name sounds like I know it," he said, playing the game.

"He's from your hood somewhere," she replied.

"Oh, shit. I think that's the Lil' nigga that has family from my hood, but he stay out south in this big ass house by my cousin."

"Naw, you must be talking about someone else named Man-Man. Man Man stays out east on 79th Oaklandon."

Uno smiled. She'd just laid it out for him. "Ohh! You talking about that Man-Man? The nigga who stay in that big ass yellow house?"

"Yellow house? Naw, he stays in the off-white one in the middle of the block."

"That nigga? Oh, I heard through the streets that he's copping major weight, but you know you can only half believe the streets. I don't think he's gettin' to the bag like that though. He probably copping a few bricks and getting fronted. Shit, that nigga probably ain't even got a hundred grand put up?" Uno probed.

Tee sucked her teeth. "Shitting me! That nigga be copping bags of dope every week from this nigga named Red," she said. "A hundred grand ain't shit." She laughed. "I done counted over 250 grand by myself when he came home one night with like four duffel bags. His money will go up and back down because he likes to stunt and buy cars."

Uno sipped his drink and smiled while taking in all the info. Tee had no idea she had laid the blueprint out for him to pay Mr. Man-Man a visit.

"So, Mr. Murrell, aka Uno, who else you be spending your time with?" she leaned on the table and asked.

"Right now, I'm just grinding hard, so, to answer your question, besides Punkin, it's the streets. Now, don't get me wrong, when I get my cash all the way right, I'ma settle down. But, right now, I guess you can say I'm in my takeover mode."

During the entire ride home, Tee couldn't keep her hands off Uno. First, she rubbed his chest. Then she started rubbing his dick, getting it hard through his slacks. By the time Uno pulled onto her street, she had just finished swallowing his nut, at the same time, cumming herself by playing in her pussy.

"Are you coming inside the house? Momma at work tonight," she said as she licked the side of her mouth.

"Tee, I would love to come in there and beat that pussy up, but I still have to make some moves before it get too late."

"Umm, when you gonna give me some of this dick? Because I'm a big girl now. I can handle all of what you have."

"Oh, yeah? Listen, we'll hook back up tomorrow."

Tee kissed Uno on the cheek and winked at him. "Alright, I'll see y'all tomorrow," she said with a grin, then hopped out.

Uno waited to make sure she got inside before pulling off.

***

As Nasty cruised the city, wondering when his time to come up was going to happen, his phone rang.

"What's up, nigga?"

"What's popping wit' you, nigga? You know a nigga just took Tee out and picked her brain."

"Oh, yeah?" Nasty asked, smiling.

"Nigga, you ain't gonna believe this shit. Peep game. Ol' dude stay right under us out east in Oaklandon. I gotta change, so pull up at LR spot," Uno said, then hung up.

Twenty minutes later, Uno was pulling up in front of LR's spot, where Nasty was sitting on top of his car. Uno hopped out and gave Nasty a dap. As they talked, they heard gunfire. Both reaching for their guns, they looked around. Nasty told Uno that LR was just in the back of the house, making a sale.

Uno grabbed the AK-47 from the bushes and ran toward the back.

"What the fuck happened?" Uno asked LR, but he wasn't able to speak. Uno grabbed the gun out of LR's shaking hands and picked up the knife as he pushed LR toward the car in the front.

"Nasty!" Uno shouted. "I need you to call the cleanup crew and tell them to hurry up and get here to clean that shit up in the back."

After Uno locked up LR's spot, they hopped in Nasty's car. Once they were safe, Uno started filling him in on all of the information he'd gathered from Tee on their way out east.

As Nasty cruised through Oaklandon, Uno called Baby J and let him in on their plans.

Uno sat up, and a smile appeared on his face when he saw the house. *Bingo!* Just as Tee said, there was on off-white house sitting on the middle with Man-Man's black Beamer, white Jaguar, and green Ram truck in the driveway.

Uno envied Man-Man for a minute. Not only did the nigga have new rides and motorcycles in the driveway, but he was also living in a big ass, half-million-dollar crib. The thing was, he'd gotten put on by his family. That was why Uno was out there getting it on his own and not counting on his brothers or cousin for a handout.

***

For the next few weeks, Uno and Nasty followed Man-Man around the city like they were investigators and learned his schedule to a T, while LR and Baby J did the same with Two-Tall. During this time, Uno had been fucking Tee and picking her brain for whatever else info he could get about Man-Man.

On the third week, Uno scheduled a meeting with Nasty, Baby J, Lil' E, LR, and Babyface at Men's Grill. The place was packed, like always, when Uno arrived. Once inside, Uno spotted everyone sitting in a back booth with their faces buried in their plates.

"Damn, nigga, what took you so long? What was you doin'?" Nasty asked.

"Shit," Uno said, looking over the menu.

"Man, it's been almost a month now," Nasty said, getting serious. "When are we gonna put shit in effect? Fuck that nigga! You know me! I will get at him in broad daylight," Nasty said.

"Listen. Everyone met each other, so we goin' to move as a family," Uno said, looking at each man.

"Me, Nasty, and Lil' E will move together, and Baby J, LR, and Babyface, y'all move together. We goin' to do this, this Friday," Uno said.

Nasty smiled. "Now that's the shit I'm talking about, nigga. Some real G-shit!" he said, nodding his head and rubbing his hands together.

"Cuz, I know you be doing your own thing out your way, but I'm trying to take over the city. I'm about to start my crew and put shit in motion. Everyone of us is from out west, so our family would be called *West Side Family*," Uno said, liking the name he'd just come up with.

Chapter 19

Friday had come quickly. Everything was moving smoothly and as planned. Uno, Lil' E, and Nasty had gone over all the details of the lick and specifics of their escape thoroughly. They had gone as far as placing additional getaway cars in the area just in case they had to split up. All three were dressed in all black with black combat Timberlands. Each was equipped with a bulletproof vest with a trauma plate in the front and back for additional safety. They had earpieces for communication purposes that reached up to a five-mile radius.

Nasty's weapons of choice were an AK-47 rifle with a hundred-round drum and a 9mm. Lil' E elected to use two twin Glock .45's and a Uzi strapped around his shoulder, and Uno kept two 9mm on his hip with two Glocks with thirty-round clips. They were equipped with enough ammunition to hold off a police department.

Meanwhile, Baby J, LR, and Babyface were entering Tru's trap spot. They heard music from the bedroom.

"Lil' cuz, I need you to stay in front while me and Babyface check the back," Baby J said as the two tiptoed toward the back. Checking all the rooms to make sure they were empty, they stood outside the last one.

"On the count of three," Baby J said, counting. When he got to two, Babyface kicked in the door. Running in, Babyface put two bullets in the female's head before she could scream.

"Get the fuck up, nigga," Baby J told Tru, grabbing him by his hair. "You already know what time it is."

"It's in the oven!" Tru said, pissing on himself.

They all walked into the kitchen, where LR was standing by the door, watching for anything moving. Tru removed the top of the oven, showcasing some bricks and sticks of money.

"Come load this shit up," Baby J said to LR and Babyface.

"Are y'all goin' to kill me?" Tru asked.

"Naw, we goin' to let you walk around and give you a chance to come back to get us," Baby J said, sliding his knife across his neck.

Uno, Nasty, and Lil' E were sitting in the car, listening to 50 Cents' *'Get Rich or Die Tryin'*, amping themselves up as they waited patiently for Man-Man to exit his crib. It was midnight, and his cars were still parked in the driveway. Anticipation was killing them. A few minutes later, the moment of truth came when Man-Man stepped out of the front door.

"This bitch ass nigga is so damn predictable," Uno said with a grin, crouched down on the ground across the street.

Man-Man exited his crib casually with a duffel bag in his hand. He never once surveyed the area as he walked over to his Ram truck.

"Let's go," Nasty said as he anxiously reached for his rifle on the ground.

"Chill, nigga," Uno said, grabbing his arm.

"Man, what the fuck?" Nasty asked, looking at Man-Man's brake lights illuminate the night.

As Man-Man backed out of the driveway, his headlights flashed on them. Man-Man's mind was so stuck on money that he never even noticed the three lying in the bushes as he pulled off.

"Fuck!" Nasty cursed as he bit the inside of his mouth, looked at Uno, and waited for him to give an explanation.

Uno laughed. "Chill the fuck out, bro. Trust me. He's going to get that pack as we speak."

"I hope you didn't just fuck this up!" Nasty said, shaking his head.

"Patience is everything. Have I never steered you wrong?" Uno asked as the three waited for Man-Man to return.

Lil' E just looked at the two with a smile on his face. He could tell the two loved each other like brothers. The plan was for the three to wait patiently until it was confirmed that Man-Man had the dope in his possession, and then they would make their move. Man-Man always left the house around this time with one bag and returned minutes later with two. He did it every week.

"Listen. When I give y'all the word that the nigga got the front door open, I want y'all to move fast, and, Lil' E, hit his ass before he gets in the house. By that time, I'll already be done made it across the street. You got me?"

"Yeah, got you," Lil' E replied.

"Good! Alright, go and post up across the street," Uno told him.

Lil' E hopped up, threw his duffel bag over his shoulder, and ran across the street, staying as low as he could to the ground. He posted up in the bushes.

"I'm here," Lil' E told the two by earpiece.

"Just sit tight, and in a minute, we will be good," Uno responded.

Nasty smiled. He was already spending money.

'Ashley going to be on my dick,' he thought to himself. 'I'll probably take her shopping or something.'

"Here we go," Uno said into the earpiece when Man-Man's truck came into view. "Wait until I give you the signal." Uno threw his bag over his shoulder as he surveyed the area, easing up as close as possible without becoming visible.

"Get ready, y'all," Uno told Lil' E and Nasty.

"Nigga, I been ready," Nasty said.

Just as planned, Man-Man exited the truck with two duffel bags in his hands.

'Bingo!' Uno thought to himself.

After locking up the truck, Man-Man quickly surveyed the block. He never spotted Uno as he casually walked toward the front door without a care in the world. He paused for a second to survey the block again and stuck his key in the top lock. Uno waited patiently.

Once Uno saw him put his key in the bottom lock, he yelled, "Go!" through the earpiece.

When Man-Man frantically looked up, all he saw was a masked man running toward him full speed with his gun drawn.

"Shit!" Man-Man cursed as he froze in place.

In a matter of seconds, Lil' E was on Man-Man and had hit him with the 9mm across the head.

"Ahh!" Man-Man screamed as his body hit the ground.

"Get that bitch ass nigga up!" Uno said, surveying the block.

Once everything was clear, Uno turned the key that was still in the lock and entered the house with his gun leading him. Nasty disarmed Man-Man, zip-tied him, taped his mouth, and then dragged his body inside.

"Boo?" a feminine voice yelled from the back.

'What the...?' Nasty thought as he paused and suspiciously looked at Uno and Lil' E.

Uno made hand signals with Nasty and Lil' E, indicating he was about to check and secure the backroom. Lil' E and Nasty nodded their heads, and Uno slowly made his way down the hallway with his gun still drawn.

Nasty had Man-Man lying in the living room, facing the wall at gunpoint, while Lil' E searched the kitchen.

'I know that voice from somewhere?' Nasty kept trying to figure it out.

Uno noticed there were two bedrooms when he walked toward the back of the house. Walking down the hallway, he was confident the voice came from the room with the TV on. He took a deep breath before checking the other bedroom first. That was empty aside from a bed and clothes. Once he secured that room, he slowly crept down the hall to the other bedroom. He paused for a minute and counted to five before violently kicking in the door.

"Ahh, shit!" a naked woman yelled as she sat up in bed and covered herself.

Uno stood frozen. "Bitch," was all Uno could get out of his mouth. He couldn't believe his eyes. There they were on a lick, and Ashley's grimy ass was sleeping with the enemy the whole time.

"Get your trash ass up!" Uno ordered, disguising his voice.

Ashley nervously jumped out of bed, butt naked. "Please don't kill me! I have two sons!" she begged.

Uno slapped the shit out of her with his pistol and violently grabbed her by the hair and threw her to the floor. "Bitch, shut the hell up!" Uno said.

Ashley nervously sat against the wall in the fetal position.

"Who else in this bitch?" Uno asked.

"Nobody," Ashley said.

"You know you dead if yo' ass lying to me," Uno said, cautiously checking the bedroom, bathroom, and the walk-in closet. "Get the fuck up, bitch!" he told her after securing the room, and Ashley hopped to her feet. Uno was glad they wore vests under their clothes, putting on a few pounds. "Move!" Uno said, poking his gun into Ashley's head as he escorted her into the living room.

'Man, I hope this nigga don't get on any tender dick shit, because I'm not going to let this ride—baby momma or not. I will put a shell in her head without thinking twice,' Uno thought to himself as he entered the living room and grabbed Ashley by the hair, making her lie face down on the ground.

He made Ashley lie next to Man-Man and wondered if Nasty had realized yet that the naked woman was Ashley by her body and tattoos. At first, Nasty thought the woman was just one of Man-Man's jump-offs until he saw the tattoo with his son's and his name on her shoulder. Steam came out of Nasty's ears, and he started violently slapping Man-Man with his pistol.

"Nigga, where the cash at?" Nasty asked, disguising his voice.

"Look, dude. You can have whatever you want. Just don't kill me or my lady. Come on! I got two kids," Man-Man said.

Bam! Uno violently hit Man-Man again, splitting his head open.

"Nigga, I don't give two fucks about you or your family! Now, this is my last time asking you," Uno said, cocking back his gun. "Where the fuck the money at, nigga?"

"Listen, man. There's fifteen bands of fish and ten pounds of hydro in those bags y'all took," Man-Man said.

Nasty gave Lil' E the nod to check the bags out.

"Bingo!" he said as soon as he opened the bags. Just as Man-Man said, there were fifteen bricks stamped with a spider symbol and ten pounds of hydro.

"Naw, nigga, I know this ain't it! You playing games, muthafucka. Where the money and jewelry and shit at?" Nasty asked, kicking him in the face. "Ah, shit, man!" Man-Man cursed. There was blood everywhere, coming from his face and head.

When Ashley tried to make eye contact, Uno kicked her, snapping her head back. "Bitch, keep your face to the ground. What the fuck you tryna see?" Uno asked.

Ashley cried like a baby. She just knew her face was swelling.

"It's a couple of grand and some jewelry in my room, but I swear to God, that's all that's here. That shit is all yours, man!" Man-Man said, praying they would let him walk away with his life.

"Go check the room. I got this in here," Uno told Lil' E and Nasty.

They headed to the bedroom while Uno started transferring the bricks and pounds to their own bags. Meanwhile, Lil' E and Nasty were in Man-Man's bedroom, thoroughly searching everything he had.

'I'ma gonna kill this bitch,' Nasty thought, tossing shit all around. He couldn't believe she would do him like that. He was out trying to put food on the table, pay the bills, and she was out fucking the enemy for free. After about five minutes of thoroughly searching, they had twenty thousand in cash, a Rolex, five diamond rings, and a nice-sized twenty-karat Cuban link chain.

'Yeah, nigga, you fuck my bitch, and I fuck you, bitch,' Nasty thought

When they walked back into the living room, Uno made eye contact with both of them, making sure everything was cool, and Nasty gave him a nod. Uno knew he was hurt, but that was the game they were in.

Ashley only cared about what the nigga had, and since Nasty was broke, she went off to the next best thing. That night, Nasty witnessed the power of a dollar. Uno had been telling him since day one that she wasn't shit but a chaser, but with her putting that pussy and head on him, he was blinded.

"Time's up!" Uno said as he checked his watch. He and Lil' E headed toward the front door. He surveyed the block, then eased out and dashed across the yard with Lil' E on his heels toward the getaway car. Uno tossed his bag in the backseat, cranked the Toyota up, and cruised up the street with his lights off. "Let's go," Uno said through the earpiece.

Nasty walked over to Man-Man and reached inside his pockets, stripped him of his last little cash, and slapped Man-Man in the head. "Didn't I tell you I wanted everything?" Nasty said.

'I know that voice,' Ashley thought as she lay face down.

Nasty backed out of the front door, closed it, and sprinted to the car.

Lil' E opened the back door. "Come on, nigga, damn!" he yelled before Nasty hopped in. Then they sped up the street.

The two's timing couldn't have been more perfect. Man-Man's lieutenant, Two-Tall, was just turning down the street, heading to Man-Man's house, when they made it to the corner. Two-Tall had called Man-Man over ten times but was unsuccessful in getting him on the phone.

"This trash bitch got my nigga's nose wide open to the point he can't handle his business. That nigga said he would hit my line when he made it back to the crib," Two-Tall said to no one as he jumped out of the car once he pulled up next to Man-Man's truck.

Meanwhile, Uno, Nasty, and Lil' E were at their spot, changing their clothes.

"Alright, bros, I'ma get these clothes and shit gone and meet y'all at the club," Uno said, giving them hugs.

"We'll see you there," Lil' E replied and hopped in the ride with Nasty as they pulled off.

Uno put all the evidence inside the car and set it on fire. He smiled at himself as he threw the duffel bags inside his car and sped off.

Two-Tall knocked when he made it to Man-Man's front door, but immediately pulled out his 9mm when the front door opened.

'What the hell?' he thought

Two Tall slowly crept into the house and then rushed over to Man-Man's side when he saw him lying on the floor in a puddle of blood with his hands zip-tied behind his back. It wasn't until he looked around the living room that he noticed Ashley's naked body wiggling on the floor with her hands tied too.

He helped Man-Man up and asked, "Damn, bro, who did this shit to you?"

"I don't know, but them bitch ass niggas gonna pay! It was three of them," he replied with a mouth full of blood. "I know I'm the only nigga in the city that been getting fish with that stamp, so put word out there, and when that stamp surfaces, we'll know it's ours! And when it do, we'll be right there," Man-Man said.

Two-Tall put his head down. "I got something else to tell you. TN got robbed and killed in the spot on 28th Clifton. We had over a hundred thousand and five bricks in that spot," Two-Tall said.

***

"What's up, my nigga? What's up?" was all Uno, Nasty, and Lil' E kept repeating as they gave everyone they knew dap while touring through the packed club, heading toward the bar where LR, Baby J, and Babyface stood.

"Hey, Lindsey, let me get a few bottles of Remy for me and my peoples!" Baby J told the bartender, handing her six one-hundred-dollar bills.

"You good?" Uno asked Nasty.

"Yeah, I'm Gucci," Nasty said in a low voice.

The bartender set their bottles on the counter and tried to hand Baby J his change. Uno let her keep it and tipped her another hundred with his number before she disappeared to help someone else.

Uno held his bottle in the air. "MOB, FOE, nigga!" Then he looked at Nasty and said, "You better be glad you found out now instead of later on down the road when you out here balling."

"Yeah, you right. But man, how can she do that to a nigga like me?" Nasty asked, shaking his head and sipping from his bottle.

"Listen. You gotta keep your composure and play the shit off like you don't know. Just go on with your day. Fuck that girl; she ain't nothing! She played herself. You paid, nigga."

"I know, but—"

"Fuck a *but*, nigga! You need to play the game until this shit blows over. Then, when the coast is clear, kick her to the curb. Just take care of the kids, feel me!" Uno said. "I know you're my big bro, but I need you to let the seeds I'm planting into your brain to grow. Whether you know it or not, your feelings can cause an all-out war, and we not ready for all that right now. You have to have your priorities right! It's gonna be chasing women, partying, smoking, drinking, or is it gonna be getting this money to the point you don't have to return to being broke? I'm gonna let you know now, bro," Uno said, looking into his eyes, "baby momma or not, if shit hit the fan, and you can't handle that chick, I'ma do it myself."

The two's eyes were locked, and they studied each other for a minute. Uno broke the stare when he grabbed Nasty by the shoulders and hugged him. "Look, I ain't tryna throw no threats or nothing about your girl, but I love you. We on now, bro!" Uno said, smiling. "I tell y'all what I'ma do. How 'bout next week, we all go out of town to get y'all mind right? Everything on me," Uno said.

"Hell yeah!" the crew all said at once.

Nasty just smiled. He felt better, knowing he still had someone in his corner.

"Let's get this money!" Uno yelled.

***

Meanwhile, Ashley was still at Man-Man's house, in the bathroom, crying, examining her swollen face. She didn't know what she was going to tell Nasty about her face. She knew he was going to fly off the map. Man-Man was pacing his living room floor, wearing down the soles of his Air Jordan Ones, fuming.

"Bro, you don't think that bitch set this shit up?" Two-Tall asked.

Thinking about it for a minute, Man-Man twisted his mouth and then said, "Nah, bro."

Two-Tall shook his head and raised his eyebrows.

"Nigga, what's that look for? I ain't slipping like that. That bitch don't know anything to set up," Man-Man said, not liking the way Two-Tall was thinking.

"Okay then," Two-Tall said, shrugging his shoulders.

When Ashley walked into the room, the two ended their conversation. "Can I please use your phone so I can call my sister to come and get me?" Ashley asked Man-Man.

"Fuck naw!" Two-Tall blurted out, and Ashley dropped her head to her chest as tears fell from her face.

Man-Man gave Two-Tall the look to chill out and walked over to where she stood. He lifted her head and looked at her face. Shaking his head, he kissed her on the cheek.

Two-Tall shook his head at the pussy-whipped show.

"Don't worry yourself. I'ma find them niggas and chop their heads off, okay?" Man-Man said, staring into Ashley's eyes.

Ashley nodded because her mind was spaced out as she tried to come up with something to tell Nasty.

Man-Man pointed to the phone that sat on top of the counter.

While Ashley made her call, Man-Man and Two-Tall were trying to think of any and everyone who had the balls to pull this off. There were no crews out on the streets deeper than theirs. Meanwhile, Ashley was begging and crying for her sister to come and get her out of that jam.

"Damn, girl, I have two kids, and I have to be at work in a few hours. If your ass can't get your shit right, then you need to stop cheating on Nasty," Ashley's sister said on the other end of the phone.

"I'll give you two hundred dollars, and I'll buy that dress you seen at the mall," Ashley bribed.

"Alright, bitch. Run your story by me real fast," Ashley's sister said.

***

It was a hard ride home for Nasty. He sat in his room in total darkness, gathering his thoughts. He wanted to kill Ashley so bad, but he would hold it together. As different scenes flashed through his mind, a car pulled up in front of the house. He walked over to the window and stared at Ashley getting out of her sister's car.

'This bitch is trash,' he said to himself, before hopping into their bed, playing asleep.

"Okay, bye, girl! That bitch had to hit me with that bottle because she knew she couldn't fuck with these hands!" Ashley yelled as she opened the front door. Ashley quietly closed the door. She had to stop to take a few breaths before walking toward the bedroom.

When she opened the door, she was surprised to see Nasty sleeping. Easing out of her clothes, she made her way toward the bathroom and hopped in the shower. During the shower, different things played in her mind. She was too young to be out there the way she was. She had kids to think about.

Nasty rolled over when he heard the shower turn on. He rubbed his temples, shaking the thoughts of killing her out of his head. When Ashley walked into the room, Nasty was lying on his back. She felt trash. She wiped away the tears before they fell from her eyes.

✝✝✝

Uno was on the phone first thing the next morning to make sure Nasty didn't kill Ashley. Even though Nasty told him he was good, Uno knew how he was, and the smallest thing she did or said would get him there. After chopping it up with Nasty for a minute, Uno hopped in the ride and cruised into the city to see what the streets were saying.

Man-Man and his crew were making noise in the city, so Uno knew word got out about the robberies and murders. He headed to New Doo because he needed a lineup. Sure enough, the minute he opened the door, all he heard was people talking about Man-Man getting robbed, Tru getting killed, and some young chick he was with in the spot. Uno didn't talk; he just sat back in the chair and listened. By 4:30 p.m., Uno had gone shopping and was back in the house, about to get some rest.

Chapter 20

The next week, Uno, Nasty, LR, Lil' E, Baby J, and Babyface were in The Clubhouse, enjoying all the fine women that walked throughout the place, looking good. As usual, on Fridays, the club was packed to capacity.

Every dancer in the building was fly, from their faces down to their toes, and their bodies were on point. It was easy to tell that whoever hired the women had an eye for bad bitches.

Niggas were everywhere, holding hands full of cash, hollering at every female that walked past. All the dancers had money growing out of their Victoria's Secret panty sets. When Uno saw how long the line was at the ATM, he laughed and shook his head. He respected the women's hustles. It made him happy to see them on the grind.

Everyone in the crew had a female dancing in front of them.

Trina's *"Drop it Down Low"* blasted through the speakers.

"Now, this is what's up!" LR yelled in Uno's ear over Trina as the goddess pulled her panties to the side so he could tip her.

Uno looked over the crew and smiled. They were all having the times of their lives. Uno and Baby J sat back in their chairs. Baby J raised his drink, and Uno did the same as he contemplated his next steps. The first thing he needed to do was find a solid connect so they could take things to the next level. He already had a solid team.

He knew that after they sold all the bricks, they would be sitting on a million or more, and he needed a better number than what Hip-Hop had.

"Can I get you guys anything?" a chubby, light-skinned, but cute bartender walked over and asked.

"Yeah, can I please get another double shot of Remy on the rocks?" Uno asked.

"What about your guys?" she asked.

Uno looked over at the crew and shook his head.

"Naw, they cool."

"Okay, I'll be back, cutie," the bartender said before disappearing behind the bar.

Uno couldn't stop glancing at the fine ass redbone with green eyes dancing for this dude in a Gucci suit. She, particularly, caught his eye. She kept locking eyes with Uno as she positioned herself on her customer's lap, grinding on him extra. Uno's dick kept jumping just from looking at her, so he knew dude felt some way. The redbone slid off her customer as she massaged the side of his face.

'The power of seduction,' Uno thought as he saw the dude hand over a handful of cash.

"Here's your drink, sir," the bartender said, setting his drink down.

Uno shook his head, shaking out of his daze. "Thank you," he said, handing her a fifty.

"I don't blame you, boo. She's the hottest in the club. Everyone comes to see her. Men. Women," the bartender said and walked off smiling. Stopping, she turned around and said, "Pray! You're gonna need it if you think what I know you're thinking!"

'Pray? She must've fell and bopped her head. I'm a fucking Uno,' he thought to himself as he sipped his drink.

She locked eyes with Uno as she sashayed his way like he was next in line. She walked right up to Uno, boldly sat down in his lap, and threw her hands around his neck. "Hey, boo. How you doing? I'm Misty," she said with a pretty smile. "You want a dance?" she asked, rubbing his body.

"Naw, I'm good, Ms. Lady," Uno said.

Misty frowned with her nose up. "What? You don't think I'm good enough for you?" she asked, standing and spinning around in a circle to show off her body.

Uno gave her a grin as he looked her up and down. Because she was up close, in his face, she was better looking. She had some pretty toes but small feet. She was thick in all the right places, and her waist was small. She had a pussy gap that was so wide that her legs wouldn't shut.

"What, nigga?" she asked as she confidently looked him up and down for an answer "You don't got nothing to say now?" She smiled.

"You look good, baby. I know you out on your hustle, and time is money, so I'm not goin' to waste any more of yours. But I will holler at you when you're not on the clock," Uno said, slouching back in his chair. "Also, that way, I can get to know the real you—not Misty," he said, handing her a hundred-dollar bill.

Misty pushed his money back toward him. "You keep your money! I don't need it, and I didn't work for it, but you did have one thing right. Time is money, so I'ma bounce," Misty said. The two just stared at one another for a minute, and then she put a smile on her face.

Misty was never the type of female who chased after niggas, but Uno's confidence immediately caught her eye. She liked the way he carried himself, and his swag was on ten. Everything about him screamed, *"That nigga,"* so she was eager to find out why.

"I tell you what," Misty said, standing in front of him. For that hundred, I will give you four dances, and that's just because I like you a little," she said, getting on top of him and riding his lap.

Every eye in the building was watching and whispering about the dude Misty was with.

Misty stared into Uno's eyes seductively for a while, making her pussy wet. She didn't know what it was, but most dudes chased her. Not Uno. She could tell he was getting money.

Uno gave Baby J a nod as he watched him and the white girl walk up the stairs toward the next level.

"You having fun?" she asked, looking down at the bulge that stood out in his slacks. The more she ground on him, the harder he got, and the wetter her pussy became. She was eager to find out who he was and what he stood for. By the end of the song, not only did Misty cum in her panties, but she knew she had to level with Uno. "Check me out. I'm going to change my clothes, and I will be back," Misty stood up and said, about to walk toward the locker room.

"Listen, baby. Don't let a nigga like myself stop you from getting this paper. These niggas are hungry, so eat," Uno said, grabbing her arm.

"First of all, I made me a few thousand. I'm Misty. I get to the bag," she said with her hands on her hips, shifting her weight. "So, are we going to Denny's or what?"

"Shit, fuck it. I'm hopping in with you?" Uno asked with a smirk on his face. "Let me holla at my peoples real fast," he said, nodding toward his crew coming down the stairs one by one.

"Don't go anywhere," Misty teased, rushing off toward the dressing room.

"Bro, they got some shit going on upstairs!" was the first thing Lil' E said when he saw Uno.

"Nigga, that was a bad bitch you were talking to. Everyone keep talking about her. Everyone said she's the coldest thing in here! I know you dropped a bankroll on her," Babyface said.

"Nigga, I'm Uno. I didn't pay the hoe shit. I gave her a little conversation, and for that, she's taking me out to eat," Uno said, laughing at the looks from LR, Nasty, lil' E, and Babyface.

"Yeah, okay," Lil' E said with a twisted mouth.

"Nigga, me and you are two different people. You see, I'm a pussy magnet. Plus, I let the hoes come to me; I don't chase them, feel me? Also, I choose who I want," Uno replied.

When Misty came from the dressing room, from the way she dressed, it was obvious that she was that bitch. Misty was Gucci'd down from her shades to her heels.

Nasty sat back and shook his head because if she had gotten to him first, she would have had every cent in his pocket. *'She is a bad bitch,'* he thought.

"We'll meet you outside in the parking lot, bro," LR said, following behind the crew.

The whole club moved in slow motion when they saw Uno strolling through the club with Misty on his arm. All the dancers were in total shock because they had never seen Misty leave with anyone.

Walking past the bar, Uno hit the bartender, who told him to pray with a nod and smile. The bartender couldn't do anything but open her mouth.

Outside in the parking lot, Uno and Misty were getting better acquainted. His sense of humor had her constantly showing off those Nu-Nu dimples. She found herself liking him more and more as he continued to talk. A man always scored points in her book anytime he held a decent conversation with her. Right at that moment, Uno was at the top of her list.

The crew came out of the club hand-in-hand with their lady friends.

"Hold on a hot second," Uno told Misty as he headed over to the crew.

Baby J and Uno drove together, so he headed over to the car. Uno grabbed his .45 caliber off the floor, but grabbed his bag to play it off like he was grabbing something out of it.

"A'ight, y'all, I'll see y'all back at the room," Uno said to the crew, headed to an awaiting Misty. Uno was immediately impressed when she hit the alarm of a brand-new Audi sitting on twenty-twos.

"What did you expect? I'm a bad bitch, so it's only right for me to have a bad ass ride to go along," she said, smirking as she unlocked the doors.

The sound of Gangsta Boo's *"Love Don't Live"* blasted through the speakers as Misty pulled out of the parking lot.

Denny's wasn't as packed as Misty thought it would be on a Friday night. The two were seated and looking over their menus in less than five minutes. After taking their orders, the waitress disappeared to the back.

"So, are you gonna let me know who the real you is?" Uno asked.

"Well, I'm from Texas. I'm twenty-two, and I have a five-year-old son named LJ. I'm single. I own my house, plus the land it's sitting on. I drive from Texas to Arizona to dance on the weekends. I can't be doing this for too long. I want to open my own business."

Uno nodded. "Impressive."

The waitress interrupted their conversation when she returned with their orders. "If there's anything else I can get for you, please, don't hesitate to ask," the waitress said.

Uno tipped her twenty. "Thank you," he said.

"Naw, thank you, and enjoy y'all meals," she said, then walked off.

While Misty cut up her sausages and pancakes, she stared at Uno with a smile on her face.

"That was nice of you to tip her," Misty said, sitting back in her seat and taking a sip of her water. "So, I know a fine ass brother like yourself isn't single," she commented.

"I have a few friends. That's about it, but this isn't about them right now," he said, eyeing her. "So, tell me the reason you came out with me," Uno said.

"It was something about the way you were staring at me that had me locked in. From the time you and your people walked in the building, I knew y'all was different than all the dudes in there. Then you stood out from your people. You walked like you owned the club, so that had me wanting to get to know you better."

"That's what's up," Uno replied, leaning back in his chair.

"Okay, then tell me what your business going to be, and what is it goin' to bring to the table that the next one doesn't have?" Uno asked.

"Hold on for a hot second," she said, flying out the door.

Uno ate a piece of steak and eggs, waiting for her to come back to the table.

"I'm sorry for holding you," she said, returning to the table with a yellow folder.

She set the folder next to Uno, and he nodded his head and listened to her every word as she flipped page after page. Misty was really on her shit.

"I'm telling you, this is gonna be something!" she said in an excited tone. "I can see it now!" Misty's," she said. "My restaurant is going to be the best. I'm already training to become a professional chef."

"I see you naming it Misty's, so what's the science behind your name?" Uno asked.

"Misty's represents leadership; the boss amongst leaders, and Jordan because I am balling on deez bitches—who's the muthafuckin greatest of all times!" she said, smiling.

"So, how much is this gonna run you?" Uno asked.

"I've been searching for a building, so I'm not sure, but off the dome, I will say about $100-$150,000."

***

"I have a good idea," Misty said as she followed him into his suite.

"What's that?" Uno asked.

"Why don't you fuck me out on the balcony?" Misty asked, walking onto it while stepping out of her clothes.

Uno raised his eyebrows as he stripped down and smiled, headed toward her.

"Open your legs," he instructed her as he tore open the rubber with one hand and held onto her with the other while she sat on the rail.

She took hold of his dick and slid it into her pussy. She held on to him tightly as he dicked her down. After a few minutes of her hanging off the rail, she jumped down so he could fuck her from the back. Misty's ass cheeks shook like Jell-O as she threw it back. She knew what she was doing.

Uno gripped her ass and slowly guided her body back toward him. His eyes were rolling in the back of his head as she looked over her shoulder at him.

"Is this pussy good? She asked, rubbing her clit.

"Oh my God!" she screamed as her juice shot out of her.

The two were so caught up that neither of them saw the couple sitting on the balcony next door to them. The couple sat back with smiles on their face as they watched the show. When Misty looked up, she and the woman smiled at each other. The woman sat in astonishment, while her boyfriend sat with his eyes wide open and tongue hanging out of his mouth, wishing he were the dude. Misty couldn't stop throwing it back; she was about to cum again.

"Don't nut without me!" Misty ordered.

Uno's eyes rolled in the back of his head again while gritting his teeth, pumping harder.

"Come on, baby," Misty told him.

"Ah shit, I'm finna -!" Uno said, busting his nut.

Misty looked at Uno and smiled. "Now that's how girls from Texas do it," she laughed.

"So, can I stay wit' you?" she asked while they walked back into the room.

Uno looked at his watch. It was 4:30 a.m. "That's on you," he replied, liking her company.

"Then I guess I'm all yours for the night," Misty said.

Chapter 21

Club Alashen Bush's parking lot was jam-packed when Uno and the crew arrived. The line was stretched a block away. Whips were valet-parked everywhere in front of the club.

"Damn! Look at all these muthafuckin people in line," LR said unbelievingly as Uno cruised the parking lot before pulling up to the valet with Baby J behind him.

"How you guys doing tonight?" the female valet asked as she opened the door for Uno and handed him a yellow ticket.

"Aye, my dude. I know they have a VIP line, right? Because we not standing in no line," LR said. The male valet nodded his head at a short, fat man wearing a suit with shades on.

"What's up, my guy? The valet said to holla at you about the VIP line," LR asked with the crew standing next to him.

"Tonight, it's a three-hundred-dollar coverage apiece," the dude said.

"Damn, apiece?" LR asked, shaking his head. Uno calmly peeled off the bills and handed them over. The man removed the black rope, giving the crew entrance.

Uno rubbed his hands together and grinned when they walked through the door of the club. "Now this is what I'm talking about," he said, admiring all the candy walking around.

The inside of the club was like a high school fashion show. Women were standing around, looking fine with their purses in hand and on their shoulders, rocking Prada, Fendi,

Gucci, and Chanel. The men were draped in expensive jewelry, looking like they stepped off the *GQ* magazine.

Uno nodded his head while looking at everyone. Niggas in Arizona were really getting to the bag. They had to step their game up. Bouncers stood throughout the club with *'SECURITY'* in white across their shirts. Uno saw tables off to the side, so he walked up to one of the bouncers and said a few words to him in his ear while sliding him some cash.

Uno and the crew were led to a VIP table. Where the table sat, they had a view of the whole club. Uno scanned the club while everyone else ordered their drinks. A group of about ten well-dressed men stood off to the side of the club, surrounding a dude sitting at the bar with heavy jewels on. Realizing who it was, Uno grinned and tapped Nasty and let him know.

Nasty stared over in awe. She was the coldest thing in the club, hands down. When the waitress set their bottles on the table, it snapped Nasty out of his daze.

When Misty turned around, she made eye contact with Uno, and he smiled at her. Misty gave him a nod toward the restrooms.

"I'll be right back, bro," Uno told Nasty, getting up and heading toward the men's room.

'Bitches!' Nasty thought, watching Misty ease toward the restroom to meet Uno.

"Hello, sexy," she said, walking up behind Uno.

"What's good?" Uno asked, spinning around.

She licked her lips while looking him up and down. *'Damn, I can eat this nigga up,'* she thought.

Uno just stood there, grinning, looking her up and down. She had on a Prada skirt with the matching handbag. Her thick thighs were toned up. "You look good," he commented while looking down at her little feet. "You a dangerous woman, I see."

"And?" she boldly asked, backing him up against the wall and grabbing a handful of his dick. "Oh, shit." She smiled. "Umm, yeah, I'm tryna see you asap."

"I'm leaving in two days," Uno said with a smirk.

"Well, I will see you before then," she said, spinning around and walking out the door.

Uno shook his head, grinned, and walked back to where the crew was. Baby J was hollering at a white girl when he returned to the table. Uno grabbed his bottle, sat down, and turned it up.

"Nigga, you been grinning the whole time ya was walking back over here, so what's that about?" Nasty asked.

"I'm just grinning at how ol' girl is. She don't care about hollering at a nigga while she's out with a nigga," he said, nodding toward the dude and his friends.

Dude and his friends were surrounded by bottles. Every last one had on jewelry, and women flocked to be next to them. Dude had to be someone, judging by the way everyone showed him love. Misty sat off to the side by herself, sipping a drink. She looked up in Uno's direction every so often to make sure he was good.

**

Knock, knock, knock.

"Room service!" a sexy voice said on the other side of the door.

He looked at the clock on the stand, and it was 7.30 a.m. Uno sat up in bed and wiped the sleep out of his eyes.

Knock, knock, knock.

"Room service!" the voice said again.

"Shit. I'm coming!" he yelled, grabbing his dick. Looking through the peephole, he saw a female staff member off toward the side with a cart full of trays, a pitcher of orange juice, and some flowers. "I ain't order no damn breakfast!" Uno said.

132

"I'm sorry I had to wake you, sir, but I have a job to do," the female replied.

Uno opened the door, making sure to keep the pistol behind the door.

"Good morning, sleepy head!" Misty said with a warm smile as she pushed the cart into the room. She glanced down at his morning wood. "Mmm, that's how ya greet people in the morning?" she asked, licking her lips.

"Why you here so early?" Uno asked.

She smiled as she prepared their breakfast. "I just wanted to surprise my friend before he went home. Come have a seat," she said, lighting the two candles on the table.

Sitting down at the table, Uno smirked, shaking his head. "How I know you wasn't sent here by your boyfriend to kill me with this food?" he asked.

Misty sucked her teeth. "I'm about to get comfortable," she said, undressing.

Uno attempted to eat his food, but Misty was so fine. He could only focus on her body.

Misty hit play on her phone, and R. Kelly came on as she started dancing for him.

Misty sat in his lap and slowly started grinding on him, rubbing over his head. The more she danced, the bigger Uno's dick grew. She licked his ear for a while, hopped up, and then walked to the bed where she lay across it seductively.

She slid her thong off while Uno walked toward her. Uno grabbed the box of rubbers off the dresser. While he opened the box, Misty grabbed his dick, locked eyes with him, and started licking the head, then took him into her mouth and sucked him like he was a sucker. Uno's eyes rolled into the back of his head. She grabbed the rubber, tore it open with her teeth, and slid it on him.

"Now, let's see who you goin' to tear this pussy up," she said, getting on all fours.

The whole time Uno was fucking Misty all over the room, Big Dawg's comment ran through his mind. While Uno was inside her, he was thinking about how he was going to fuck her mentally. Uno was dicking her down like it was the last pussy on earth. With each stroke, Misty's walls expanded to accommodate Uno's dick.

'Damn! This nigga must've popped a pill,' Misty thought to herself.

Uno walked her back to the bed, where he flipped her like a pancake until he nutted. Uno grinned and headed to the shower.

***

"Somebody owes me some muthafuckin answers!" Man-Man said, pacing the living room of one of his spots. "It's been almost two weeks, and nothing. Someone robbed and killed Tru, and y'all not out there tryin' got find out who. What type of niggas are y'all? I don't get it," Man-Man said, shaking his head. "Get my money and dope!" Man-Man ordered his crew.

They all nodded their heads.

Chapter 22

The next day, Uno and the crew arrived back in the city, ready to put in work. The crew had fun in Arizona and was happy to finally be able to get some money.

"I'm gone, y'all. I had fun, but it's time for me to shoot back my way," Baby J said, giving everyone love before hopping in his car.

After dropping Nasty off at the crib, Uno headed to go check on his mother and sister since he hadn't been around. Once he pulled up to his mother's, he saw Big Dawg chilling on the porch of the house across the street.

"What's good, bro?" Big Dawg asked.

"Shit, chilling, trying to get to the bag. You know how it was when y'all was out here," Uno said, lighting up a blunt.

"You don't have to do any of this shit. Why do ya think me and Ant did it for so you wouldn't have to, but you your own man, and can't nobody tell your big head ass nothing," Big Dawg said, laughing.

After Uno chopped it up with his brother about the fun he had in Arizona, he headed over to their mother's crib. He watched his mother move around as she cooked and cleaned. Walking up to her, he gave her a hug and a kiss, then sat at the table

"Hey, son," she said, greeting him.

"I put some money in the bank for lil' sis, too, a few days ago," he said.

"She just came in the house. She's in her room; go check on her. She would be happy to see you," she told her son.

Uno stood in his sister's doorway and smiled as he watched her stretch across her bed and talk on the phone.

"I'm gonna call you back. What's up, bro?" she asked, looking up at him.

"I put some money in your bank account a few days ago, so make sure your grades stay up because you off to college in a few years," Uno said.

"Thank you, bro." She stood up and hugged him. "Y'all stay blessing me with stuff." She smiled. "Y'all the best brothers in the world," she said, meaning every word.

"Listen, lil' sis. Momma got three boys in the game. We be stressing her out, so we need you to get her up out of here, and goin' off to college is going to do that," Uno said, hugging his sister.

When Uno walked back into the kitchen, his mother had the table set for five with yellow rice, collard greens, baked macaroni and cheese, fried chicken, and deviled eggs. Big Dawg, Ant, and their little sister all walked in behind Uno and sat down to have dinner. For the next twenty minutes, the five socialized and joked like a family. Uno was big on family. After dinner, Uno kissed his mother and little sister and headed out the front door.

Uno was so exhausted when he arrived at his apartment that he didn't even bother grabbing his things from the car. He headed into the house and went straight to the shower. Punkin left him a few messages on his voicemail, letting him know she and Pooder were having fun, chilling with her aunt in ATL.

***

On the other side of the city, Nasty was chilling at the IMAX theater with LR's female friend's sister named Tay-Tay. This was their fourth date. The two had dined at the all-you-can-eat Chinese place earlier and were vibing at dinner. It was astounding how much they had in common. Tay-Tay had really taken Nasty's mind off the troubles Ashley had been causing him.

Tay-Tay rested her head on Nasty's shoulder because the hydro they smoked before walking into the movies had her eyelids heavy.

"You're fine, you know that?" she asked, licking her lips while looking at his face.

"Who? Me?" Nasty asked with a smile.

Tay-Tay rubbed Nasty's inner thigh with a devilish grin and started stroking his dick.

"I'm ready to give you some of this good, good," she said, pulling his dick out and bending down to lick his head.

Nasty quickly scanned the theater to see if anyone saw what she was doing. He tilted his head back and started rubbing her ass while she did her thing. His hand worked its way under her dress, and before long, he was finger fucking her.

Tay-Tay moaned cries of joy, grinding on his fingers. Nasty couldn't believe she was sucking his dick. He was with the shits. They didn't call him Nasty for no reason, and she was sure to find out.

"Get up here and ride this dick," Nasty told her, pulling his dick out of her mouth.

Sitting in his lap, she began to ride his dick, moaning loudly, grabbing the attention of people in the theater. Tay-Tay rubbed on her clit while watching everyone look at the fucking in the back. By that point, all in the theater were on their feet, clapping, cheering, eating popcorn, or yelling for them to stop.

"Security is on their way!" Nasty heard someone yell from the door.

"Oh, shit!" Nasty moaned, ready to nut.

"Oh my God! I'm cumming," Tay-Tay said as she watched security walk into the theater.

After cumming together, they hopped up and ran toward the exit.

Chapter 23

Punkin and Pooder walked out of the airport with everyone else, looking for her ride. She spotted Uno leaning on the car and smiling.

"Baby, I'm glad we home because we missed you," Punkin said, hugging and kissing Uno on the lips.

"Baby, I'm glad y'all home, too, and I know y'all tired from y'all ride, but I have a surprise first," he said, putting her bags into the car.

"What you up to, boo?" she asked, looking at him suspiciously as she eased into the car.

"You'll see," he said, smiling.

Twenty minutes later, Punkin let out a sigh of relief when Uno pulled up into a lot and parked. It was a shopping plaza out in Speedway. There was a shoe store, low bills, and another building with newspaper covering the windows.

"You taking us shopping?" she asked.

"Naw, woman. Just get out and follow me," Uno said, laughing at her. Uno walked up to the building that had covers over the windows.

"Here we go," he said.

Punkin looked through a crack in the window. "Ahh, baby! This is cute!" she said, turning around to see Uno smiling.

Looking harder, she caught an attitude. "I know damn well these muthafuckas ain't get their place set up just how I would like my shit," she said.

"I said the same shit when I saw the place," Uno said, knocking on the window of the place.

A black lady in her late thirties opened the door and welcomed them inside. Punkin looked her up and down with fire in her eyes. At that moment, Punkin wanted to slap the shit out of the woman.

"Mr. Brandon, how are you today?" Kerry asked, shutting the door behind them.

"I'm fine, Kerry," Uno hugged her and said.

"And this must be Ms. Brew and Pooder?" Kerry asked with a smile.

Punkin looked at her with a crazy look, and Kerry gave her a puzzle look in return.

Uno saw the exchange, so he intervened. "Baby, I'd like you to meet your assistant manager."

"Nice to meet you," Punkin said, shaking her hand, lost.

Uno knew she was lost, and he wanted to laugh so badly, but he kept it together. Uno decided to enlighten her by handing her a set of keys and the deed. "This is all yours. All you have to do is give it a name, and you'll be good to go," he said.

"Oh my God! No, you didn't!" she yelled, jumping into Uno's arms.

"Care for a tour of the place?" Kerry asked.

***

"Man, this shit is crazy! I can't believe this bullshit! A few weeks ago, we were serving niggas bricks, and now we sitting on the fucking block hand-in-hand," Two-Tall said as he sat at the table, cutting and bagging up rocks.

Man-Man was sitting at the table in a daze. He hadn't been at this level since his cousin put him on a few years back. It was fucking him up that in a matter of a few weeks, his life had changed for the worse. Of the bricks he got robbed of, only seven were his, and the rest, his plug fronted him, so he had to sell his bikes and cars so he could get his connect the money. To make matters worse, his connect wasn't fucking with him anymore after the robbery. Since he was dead broke, he couldn't afford to pay for the big house he was staying in, so he had to move in with his sister.

"Damn, nigga, you good over there?" Two-Tall asked him.

Man-Man snapped out of his daze. "I can't do this small-dog shit. We gotta hurry up and find a new connect to front us a couple of bricks until we can bounce back. If we don't, we gonna lose everything we worked hard to build."

"I feel you, bro. You know your men Uno and LR been making a lot of noise in the streets. Word in the city is them niggas got that shit," Two-Tall said.

"Oh, yeah?" Man-Man sucked his teeth and asked.

***

Uno and LR were cruising around the city, trying to find houses for them to set up shot in.

"You know what, bro? Ride down Eugene," LR said with a smile.

As Uno cruised down Eugene, LR had a smile on his face the whole time. A group of niggas were posted up and down the block. Stopping Man-Man out there, he pulled up beside him and rolled down his window.

Man-Man stood back, and all of his crew reached for their waists.

"Man-Man, what's good, bro? I didn't know you was still huggin' the block," Uno said, easing out the car behind LR.

"What's good, nigga?" LR asked, giving him dap.

"Shit, we out here trying to get it in every which way," Man-Man said.

"Well, we was just cruising around the hood, so I thought I would swing by to hit you back for the love you showed me when I first got home. I'm up now, so right on," he said, reaching into his pocket and pulling out a wad of hundreds so big that it looked like he had a softball in his hand. He peeled off thirty hundred-dollar bills and handed it to Man-Man, who hesitantly took the bread.

"I got something for you, too," LR said, grabbing something out of the car. "Here is a zip. Try it out because we got that on deck," he said, handing him the Ziplock bag.

Uno smiled while talking to Man-Man. "The last time I saw you, bro, you was up. It's not like you to be out here on the block, so this what I'm gonna do. Here's my number if you need me. Matter of fact, come holler at me off to the side," Uno said, stepping off so only Man-Man could hear him.

"You see, you tried to play me when I came home, but I'm gonna leave you with this. I take your money, fuck your bitches, and spend your own money on her." Uno walked off with a smirk, then drove off, laughing loudly.

"Bro, what you say to that nigga back there?" LR asked, knowing how funny Uno was going to be.

"Nigga I told him, I take your money, fuck your bitches, and spend your own money on her," Uno said, shaking his head.

"You hell, bro," LR said.

"Naw, I didn't tell you. When I came home, he pulled up on me and did some disrespectful shit. He gave me some cash then said if I need a job, to holler at him," Uno said, really shitty.

"What!" was all LR could say.

Chapter 24

For the past few hours, Uno and Baby J had been in the kitchen, whipping up bricks. It was Friday morning, and they were in the spot, smoking on the best, waiting for all the dope to dry up. Ever since he learned the whip game from his brothers, Uno had been killing the city, charging eight hundred dollars a zip, bringing $28,800 off each brick. But then they busted down a whole brick and put fives, tens, and twenties in a spot. Uno remembered when he first cooked some dope and lost.

Man-Man was still on the hunt for who robbed him and killed his lil' homies. He knew he was the only nigga in the city with fish scale, so he was sitting back and watching, waiting for the bricks to resurface. Something in his gut told him Uno had something to do with it.

Uno had been taught by the best the city had seen. His brothers weren't moving work anymore, but they still had their hands in the streets. But they gamed him up. He'd already copped a few bricks of oil to mix with the fish scale so the dope would change colors. Even though the crew was sitting on bricks, Uno still went out and copped off Hip-Hop. They were ass sticking to their normal routines and staying under the radar, and that was what was going to keep them ahead of everyone else's crews.

Once all the dope was dry, Uno separated everyone's dope. Since Uno and Baby J were doing all the work, everyone decided they would get a bigger cut. Thanks to their whip game, every brick was coming back as two.

Hearing voices outside, Uno grabbed his pistol and peered through the curtains to see. Seeing LR, Lil' E, Nasty, and Babyface getting out of their car, he let out a sigh of relief.

When they walked through the front door, Lil' E and Babyface's heads started spinning, seeing that much dope. They had dope scattered all over the house. Uno set two bags on the table, followed by Baby J.

"Today, y'all life stepped up a few levels. Now, Baby J isn't part of our crew, but he's still family. From today on, we will be called *The Westside Family*, WSF for short," Uno said, pushing his two bags in front of Lil' E and Babyface.

Lil' E opened his bag, looked inside, and shut his eyes. Uno just looked with a smirk on his face. He knew his little homie was about to get to the bag.

"That's ten bricks a piece at thirty-five thousand apiece. There's no way you shouldn't walk away with $350,000 apiece, and when y'all down, put up some bread, bring some back to the table, and we do it all again."

Babyface stood there, speechless. His eyes had never seen that much dope in his life. "These niggas are in trouble; it's about to be a takeover," he said.

"Nasty!" Uno yelled.

"What it do, nigga?" he asked, walking into the kitchen.

"Bro, you been home for a little while now, so you been waiting on this come up. The thing is, what you gonna do with this moment?" Uno asked.

***

By the time night hit, Uno had already run through ten bricks of crack. After serving his weight clientele, he drove around before making a pitstop out post. Kode Red was the last person he had to serve.

"What's good with ya, Kode Red?" Uno asked.

143

Kode Red pulled out a wad of cash. "Let me get a half brick."

Uno pulled out sixteen ounces and handed it to him.

"Lil' bro, you know, you don't have to keep coming out this way to serve these niggas. You can hit me with a brick or two, and I can serve them. Feel me, blood?" Kode Red said.

"I tell you this. Here's a whole one. Just gave me twenty-six thousand in a few days."

Kode Red smiled and gave him dap. "You a solid nigga! That's showing love! I'll have that bread for you in the morning, though, because I'm about to hug the block," he said, hopping out of the car.

Uno honked his horn and headed to Greenwood. For the rest of the night, he cruised the city, dumping work on niggas. By eleven o'clock, he had $150,000 to put on the table. They were seeing a lot of money, but it was time for them to step up their game. A solid connect was what he really needed to take his crew to the next level.

Punkin's place was just his first investment of money to come for him and his loved ones. His plan was to have everyone in the family open something up. That way, they could wash some of the money they were making.

Uno was planning to help Misty open up her spot as well. They had talked on the phone many times since Uno had come back to the city. He talked to her the night before and agreed to hit her with half of the money she needed to get the ball rolling for her spot. Besides, he had never been to Texas and wanted to peep out their city. He had a plan, and it was much bigger than the city of Indianapolis.

Chapter 25

A week later, Misty drove around Dallas, Texas, showing Uno the town. The two had connected on so many different levels that it scared Misty. She was enjoying his company and was hurt when he told her he was headed back home the following day. It really messed her mind up when she found out that Uno wasn't even eighteen years old.

That previous night, they enjoyed dinner at a five-star restaurant, but that night, Misty was taking him to a different atmosphere she thought he'd like.

"So how are you liking Texas so far?" Misty asked.

"Listen, Misty. I'ma be honest with you. This is a cool city and all, but I'm a hood nigga. I want to go to the hood and see the niggas that's hugging the block," Uno said, puffing on his blunt.

Misty made a few turns, and they made it to the hood.

Uno nodded his head as they drove down the block. "Now this my type of shit," he said, watching everybody who hugged the block get money.

Misty took Uno to one of her family member's cribs to cop some dro, and then she swung by Get Down soul food to give him a good idea of how down south soul food tasted. After they ate dinner, she decided to take him to the strip club. Uno smiled and shook his head when she pulled into the parking lot.

Inside, the club was packed. Uno felt like he was at one of the spots in Indianapolis, based on how dudes were acting around all the females dancing and performing tricks.

"I want you to meet a few females," she told Uno, leading the way through the crowd.

Everybody showed Misty love like she was famous, but Uno liked it because once she opened her restaurant, it would help.

Misty motioned for the bartender as they sat down at a table.

"Hey, Misty." The bartender greeted her with a hug. "Girl, I can't wait to quit this bullshit ass club, so you need to hurry up and open up that restaurant," she said.

"It's coming soon, Kandi," Misty said. "Do me a favor. Tell London, Khloe, and Nicki that I'm here. By the way, this is my partner, Uno," Misty said.

"Nice to meet you," Kandi said, extending her hand.

"Likewise." Uno shook her hand and flirted with his eyes.

Kandi looked at Misty and saw the look on her face, so she hurried to slide her hand away from Uno and rushed off to grab the girls.

Misty looked over at Uno, who had a grin on his face. "You're a mess!"

Uno laughed.

Three bad women with banging bodies walked over to the table and gave Misty hugs, then they sat down at the table. One at a time, each woman gave Uno a handshake.

"Every female I'm showing you is going to work for me. I have to bring sex appeal," Misty said. With the introductions out of the way, Misty took Uno over to another club to show him Iggy. "There she go, right there on stage," Misty said, pointing at a white girl as they walked through the club.

They both sat at a table, ordered some drinks, and watched Iggy do her thing on the pole. Iggy was the spitting image of the white girl from the show called *The Parkers*. She stood about five-ten and weighed roughly around 160 pounds. Her 32DDDs and fat ass looked like they belonged to a black girl.

"And that's her real body. But what's so crazy is she's doing this to pass time."

After Iggy walked off the stage, Misty stood and motioned for her.

"Hey, girl." Iggy came over and hugged her.

"Iggy, I'd like for you to meet Uno. He's my partner," Misty said.

"Damn, girl, you got a fine partner!" Iggy said.

"Watch it, bitch. He's taken," Misty joked, but she was so for real.

Iggy and Uno shook hands, then she sat down. After they talked and came to a mutual agreement, Iggy had to get back on stage to do her solo.

The ride to Misty's house was a bumpy one. She had gotten used to Uno around. She felt like she had found a man who was on her level and had the same drive as herself. She looked over at Uno, who was lying back with his eyes closed.

Chapter 26

After a heavy night of sex, Uno and Misty were at the airport, saying their goodbyes. Neither one of them wanted the weekend to end. It was sad to say they had so much fun. Misty stood before Uno and nervously bit her bottom lip.

"I had fun this weekend," Uno said, looking into her eyes.

"I wish you could stay, or I could go with you," she mumbled with her head down. She felt like a little girl under Uno's gaze. She'd never felt like this about any dude in her life. Uno had her nose wide open from his dick game to his swag.

"Maybe you can come up and see my city," Uno whispered before kissing her lips.

Misty stood motionless and waved goodbye as tears poured down her face.

By ten o'clock, Uno was up in the air, enjoying watching the clouds as he thought about his life. He'd been enjoying the females in his life. Misty really showed him a good time. She was older than him, but she had her head on right, and she was chasing that money train, like him. He loved Punkin, and no female could take that, but right then, she had to understand his grind. He didn't think the game was for life. His goal was to get enough money so he and those around him could do as they pleased. His last few trips out of town really opened his eyes to bigger and better things.

***

Uno's flight landed in Indianapolis a little before six p.m., and LR and Nasty were waiting for him when he came walking out the door. "How was your trip, bro?" Nasty asked, giving him dap.

"Gucci. Ol' girl is on her shit," Uno replied with a smile.

"I made up some flyers for Punkin's, so we about to head to Riverside to pass them out," LR said.

"'Bout time you using that big ass head for something," Uno joked, putting his luggage in the car.

The streets of Indianapolis were filled with life when they arrived back in the city. It was a beautiful, warm Sunday night, and Riverside looked like a car show. Anybody who was somebody from all of the surrounding counties headed to Riverside to show out and stunt hard.

"Damn, this bitch is fat out here!" Nasty said as he pulled his Porsche rental into the park's parking lot.

Females from the city were out and representing Indianapolis hard. All the crews were out, wandering the parking lot, looking fine. This was their city and stomping grounds, so they weren't about to let some hoes from out of town outshine them and take their niggas.

Uno, LR, and Nasty swagged through the crowd, passing out flyers for the grand opening of Punkin's spot. The way the three of them were moving, one would have thought they owned the city.

"Yo, cuz, look at them niggas!" Man-Man said, watching them talk to a lot of their clientele.

"Them niggas ain't on shit! Nigga, I'm in a brand-new Lamborghini truck. You think I'm worried about them three niggas who riding around in a Porsche rental?" Man-Man's cousin asked, sipping his drink.

Man-Man's cousin and his whole crew smiled, but Two-Tall didn't think it was a game, especially since a lot of their clientele had been buying dope from Nasty and LR for the past few days.

Man-Man went and posted on his sister's Toyota, watching the three give everyone love. Man-Man sipped his drink as he shook his head. He wasn't himself. Just a while back, he came through in a Jaguar and had all the work. He just looked off into space and wondered where things went wrong for him and his crew.

"Bro, them niggas are making moves in the streets," Two-Tall told Man-Man. "You still be dicking down that nigga Nasty's BM?" he asked.

"Yeah, the bitch been acting real funny, though," Man-Man said.

"I know that bitch is strapped, though," Two-Tall said, grabbing his dick.

Man-Man looked at him sideways.

"Bro, you need to stop playing and put your ego to the side and ask that nigga to hit you off with some work," Two-Tall said. "The way that half brick just moved, we can see if he would let us buy one and front us the other one."

"I'll see what's up. I gotta take my sister her car back because she has something to do. Let's bounce," Man-Man said.

Uno, LR, and Nasty were posted up, watching all the cars and bikes doing tricks as they stunted. Uno could tell by the way LR kept looking at the cars and bikes that he wanted one so badly. LR and Nasty just looked on as women flocked to the niggas in tight ass cars.

Nasty was wondering why Uno hadn't gone out and copped something silly because he knew he was sitting on bands.

"So, bro, when we all gonna go out and cop us something?" LR asked Uno.

"We ain't tryna impress anybody. When it's time, we will shine. I promise," Uno said.

"All these same dudes out here stunting been copping bricks from us these last few days. All these bitches is all over them niggas Beeper and his crew, like they the thing,"

LR said, looking at Beeper and his crew. "Shit, I was just thinking about goin—"

Uno cut him off mid-sentence. "Think! Every path you take leads up to a choice. Some choices change your whole life. You tryna move too fast. It hasn't been that long since we hit dude, so if you go out throwing money every which way, niggas goin' to talk," Uno said.

"You right, bro." LR just shook his head, then mean-mugged Beeper as he gritted his teeth. "Me and Two-Tall had a few words the other day, but it ain't nothing."

"Why am I just now hearing this, and it's more to it," Uno said, knowing LR. "Tell me everything."

"Alright, I was a little arrogant, but that nigga came out of his mouth sideways, talking about I'm out of bounds. I told him to respect the hustle and step his game up. Then he continued to talk slick, saying he put blood, sweat, and tears in this and was willing to go to the end about his. So, you know me, I let it be known it's a difference in walking this street life and only knowing about the life, feel me! It wasn't shit, though. I laughed at him and sped off," LR said.

Chapter 27

The day marked the grand opening of Punkin's restaurant, barber shop, and salon. It was a sunny, beautiful Saturday afternoon, and Hot 96.3 was broadcasting live outside. Inside the restaurant was jam-packed. It seemed like every female in the city came out to show Punkin support. All the ballers across the city even showed up to sweat all the women and get their eat on.

Punkin looked over at Uno standing off, and she blew him a kiss. Tee waved at him from a table. He looked around at the restaurant, barber, and salon shop and felt proud of Punkin and himself. The three shops were on point. He winked at his sisters from his mom and pops side. His mother, brothers, and cousins lifted their glasses to show him love. Uno mingled with the patrons who were taking advantage of the free food, wine, haircuts, and hairdos.

Ashley and Tee made eye contact when Ashley walked into the restaurant. Tee took a few deep breaths and tried to remain professional as Ashley continued to stare at her.

"Would you like water or wine?" Kerry asked Ashley.

"Wine," Ashley replied with a smile. "May I use your restroom?"

Kerry pointed to the side where the restroom was, and Ashley headed in that direction.

"I have to handle something," Tee said, excusing herself from her table.

Meanwhile, Ashley was inside the bathroom, pacing the floor. "I came to treat myself to a meal and hairdo, and I bump into this bitch?" she said, checking herself in the mirror. It had been a while since her run-in with Tee. Ashley took a few deep breaths and exited the bathroom. She smiled when she saw Tee posted on the wall outside the bathroom.

"Didn't I tell you when I saw you, it was on, bitch?" Tee asked, rushing into Ashley's face.

Ashley surveyed the area but saw they were alone. "Listen, I don't even mess with Man-Man. He told me he didn't have a girlfriend, and I believed him because he took me to his house," she said as Tee blocked her into the corner.

"What the fuck is goin' on here?" Uno bent the corner and asked.

"This the chick that I caught Man-Man creeping with that one day!" Tee said, staring Ashley down like she wanted to tear her head off.

Ashley looked into Uno's eyes and dropped her head.

"I wouldn't have came if I knew you worked here," Ashley said in a pitiful voice.

"Work? Bitch, I own my shit," Tee said. Uno looked at Ashley and smiled. The plan fell perfectly. Now, Nasty could kick Ashley to the curb.

"Listen, this is my BM business, so y'all gonna have to handle this somewhere else because, right now, y'all fucking with my paper!" Uno said.

***

On the other side of the city, traffic had started booming at one of Man-Man's spots. Slowly but surely, Man-Man and Two-Tall had worked themselves back up to two bricks.

With Uno offering to hit Man-Man with whatever, Man-Man's ego was too big and wouldn't let him ask for the handout. He refused to let Uno and them see him down bad, so he only copped whatever his money would let him.

Fat D pulled up on the block and stepped out of the car, looking like money. Fat D was the fat, brown, skinny, pretty boy with colorful eyes. He kept a fresh fade and the newest shoes. He'd been in the spot for days, grinding hard, putting money in Man-Man's and Two-Tall's pockets. He was so tired, and he needed a break.

"Damn, bro, who faded you up?" Man-Man asked.

"Man, I'm coming from Punkin's, Uno's new spot. You niggas gotta see that shit for y'all selves. I'm talking about something you would see on TV. They have a restaurant, a barber shop, and a salon all connected in one! They even got waitresses serving people wine or water for free! And the bitches? Oh, God, the bitches came to show out!" he said. "I seen that fine ass chick you used to fuck with, Man-Man. Both of them. Punkin and Tee. With a spot like that, y'all know they about to get a bag," he said, laughing, and the whole crew joined him.

Man-Man was shitty, so he got in his feelings.

"Them niggas ain't about to do shit," Man-Man said, getting in Fat D's face.

Everybody shut up. At first, Fat D blew it off as he was bullshitting until he saw the seriousness on Man-Man's face. He stood his ground with his chest poked out, not backing down. The two stared into each other's eyes.

"Nigga, what the fuck is wrong with you?" Two-Tall asked, separating the two before they came to blows.

Man-Man walked away, hopped in his rental, and sped off down Edgemont. Two-Tall just stood there, looking at the rental while shaking his head. Man-Man was his bro, but sometimes, he would get on some bitch shit.

"Man, that nigga been playing crazy lately!" Fat D said. "He wanna bump with me because I'm talking about a nigga and bitch that ain't even thinking about him! He pulled that hoe ass shit with me like I'm one of these hoes! I'm the one in the spot grinding hard, selling all the dope!" he said. "Shit, that nigga ain't the boss like he used to be. We're the ones keeping that nigga above water!" Fat D said, pointing at the crew.

Two-Tall sat back and studied everyone's faces one by one. Fat D had just said what the whole crew was thinking.

"All y'all niggas feel the same way?" Two-Tall asked.

"Hell yeah," everybody agreed.

Two-Tall grinned and nodded his head in response.

"That nigga watered down!" Fat D added.

Two-Tall narrowed his eyes and walked over to Fat D. "What did you just say?"

"You heard what I said," Fat D said.

Two-Tall's six-foot-two, 220-pound frame looked down on Fat D's five-eleven frame. When Fat D didn't back down, the entire crew stared in awe at him for his courage. Every last one of them knew Two-Tall was a killer and a good fighter. Two-Tall just stared into Fat D's eyes, searching for a bit of fear. Finally, Two-Tall smiled and stepped back. He respected Fat D for not backing down from him.

"Do y'all thing! Don't let no one hold y'all back!" Two-Tall told the crew.

Fat D headed to the car, laughing and shaking his head. He stopped before getting into the car to see what the rest of them were going to do. One by one, they all followed in Fat D's direction while Fat D and Two-Tall stared at each other the whole time.

"So, you the new boss, huh?" Two-Tall asked Fat D.

"I been the boss, just not in y'all eyes," Fat D said, hopped in the car, and pulled off.

Two-Tall stood on Edgemont in total disbelief as he watched Fat D's rental. He never thought he would see the day he and Man-Man would be broke or hugging the block again. They watched so much money and dope go through their hands.

"Hey, Two-Tall, you got something for this ten?" a crackhead walked up and asked him.

Two-Tall just shook his head and headed inside the house to grab the dope and put his next move together.

***

Fat D and his crew were cruising the city, puffing blunts and passing a bottle around, listening to a Boosie's CD. Everybody was hoping Fat D had a game plan to make them some money.

"So where do we go from here?" one of the crew members asked, breaking the silence.

Everybody nodded their heads.

"Who we gonna get some work from?" the same person asked.

"Listen, bro, I'm—" He stopped midsentence when he spotted Uno and LR pumping gas at the gas station on 29th and MLK. He looked over to make sure it was them before pulling into the parking lot.

LR stood by Uno with his pistol down on his side while Uno pumped the gas.

"Niggas, don't be pulling up on niggas like that. You almost got your shit shot up," LR schooled him, surveying the area before putting his gun in his hip.

Fat D was from the Land also, but he'd been fucking with Man-Man for a while now. When Red came to the hood, Man-Man's cousin had already put him on, so he was making a little money, so Red cuffed him, knowing Man-Man would help him move his dope.

Fat D hopped out the rental. "Let me holler at y'all, bro!"

Uno looked at LR and then inside the car.

"What's good?" Uno asked.

"Check, dog, I know we never done business before, but I need y'all help. Me and my crew just had words with them niggas Man-Man and Two-Tall today, so we on some *fuck them*. We tryna to set up shop and get our own thing going, but we ain't got nobody to get on from."

Uno grinned and wrote down his and LR's numbers and handed the paper to Fat D.

"We got y'all," LR said.

The two gave Fat D dap before hopping in the car and speeding off.

The moment Fat D got in the car, the crew was on him.

"What he say?" one asked Fat D.

Fat D grinned. "We got ourselves a connect now!" he said.

For the next few hours, Fat D cruised the city, searching for a spot to set up shop. Every good location in the city was taken. Fat D drove around in deep thought as he turned down Edgemont, just to go see what Man-Man's and Two-Tall's spot was doing. Fat D shook his head as he thought about how it was them who were carrying Man-Man and Two-Tall this whole time. They had the work, but Fat D had the crew. A thought popped into Fat D's mind as he looked at the 'For Sale' sign in the yard of the house across the street from Man-Man's spot.

Chapter 28

Fat D spent all night grinding hard. That way, he had some bread to spend on himself and his crew. Around noon the next day, Fat D was handing the landlord the first and last month's rent in exchange for the keys to the house. After talking to the landlord for another twenty minutes, Fat D picked up the crew and headed to Dollar Tree to grab everything they needed to clean the house up. He had already called Uno and would meet up with him to get on.

Back in the hood, on Edgemont, Man-Man and Two-Tall were chilling in the front yard of their spot, trying to figure out their next move. Business was slow for them, and it had been like that ever since they hit the block with no crew. They were forced to hug the block themselves.

Man-Man was in deep thought, thinking about Ashley and the words she laid on him. Man-Man was really starting to second-guess Two-Tall's love and loyalty. He didn't know if Two-Tall set things up for him to get robbed. He was the only person who knew his moves, but why would he be sitting in front of their spot, acting broke?

"Check this shit out," Two-Tall said, nudging Man-Man in the arm when he spotted Fat D's rental turn onto Edgemont.

"Them niggas probably ain't got nowhere to go," Two-Tall said, smiling.

When Fat D pulled up and parked on the other side of the street.

Man-Man and Two-Tall walked to the front gate and watched Fat D hop out with the crew following him. The grin Two-Tall had on his face disappeared when Fat D looked their way and continued to walk up the stairs of the house. He walked up to the 'For Sale' sign and pulled it from the ground.

Man-Man and Two-Tall stood there in disbelief. Before Fat D could get the key in the door, a crackhead called his name.

"Hey, boo, you know I only deal with you!" the crackhead said. "Them lame ass niggas across the street said they had me, and you wasn't coming out the house today," she added, rolling her eyes at Two-Tall and Man-Man. "Anyways, I just got a trick with a fat check, so hit me off for this three hundred," she said, handing the fistful of money to him.

"You can go in the house," Fat D said, pushing the crackhead toward the house when he saw Two-Tall walking out of the yard.

"What the fuck y'all little niggas think y'all about to do over there?" Two-Tall asked, standing next to Man-Man.

"We don't want no problem. We just doing us," Fat D said, smirking.

Fat D locked eyes with both men and then backed up toward his spot. That entire night, the trap boomed. When Fat D started giving out samples, crackheads were coming out of nowhere. Two-Tall and Man-Man watched in disbelief at how all the crackheads were loyal to Fat D and his crew. They'd been sitting in the same spot all day and still hadn't made half of what Fat D had made.

Fat D and his crew were inside the house, laughing their asses off as they watched the silly looks on Man-Man's and Two-Tall's faces every time they made a sell. Fat D knew there was smoke in the air, but he wasn't backing down from anybody.

Chapter 29

The WSF operation was moving according to plan. Hiding behind Nasty's tinted windows, Uno and LR patiently waited in the parking lot for Hip-Hop to pull up on Nasty. Late that night before, Uno, Nasty, and LR had put a plan together, hoping to cut out the middleman. The money they'd been spending along with Hip-Hop, they all felt they should've been talking to the plug. Hip-Hop was one of the niggas that happened to know someone that knew someone. He wasn't a real street nigga.

Uno and LR grew impatient as they sat across the street, puffing a blunt. They called Hip-Hop that night and ordered five bricks. Uno let Hip-Hop know that he and LR would be heading out of town, so he had to pull up on Nasty, who had the money waiting for him. Hip-Hop was okay with the arrangement and agreed to pull up on Nasty around 4 p.m., but it was already 4:20 p.m. at that moment.

As soon as Uno looked at his phone, Hip-Hop's Cadillac pulled into Nasty's apartment complex. Hip-Hop hopped out of his truck, surveying the area before walking up to Nasty's door and knocking a few times.

The whole time Uno watched Hip-Hop, all he could do was shake his head at how ugly he was.

Nasty opened the door and let him inside before he stuck his head out, surveying the area. He gave them a nod, letting them know he saw them.

Uno and LR sat there, listening to Young Dro as they smoked another blunt and waited. Ten minutes later, Hip-

Hop exited the apartment with a Walmart bag with some cleaning supplies hanging out before hopping in his car and pulling off.

Uno eased into traffic, making sure to stay a few cars behind Hip-Hop. Uno tailed behind Hip-Hop until he hopped on the highway.

"This nigga must be heading to Anderson," Uno said to LR as he pulled over to the side of the road and opened the laptop that was sitting in his lap. He switched the laptop on, and a big green dot showed on the screen.

That night, when Uno, LR, and Nasty were counting out the money to give to Hip-Hop, they decided it would be smart to put a GPS in the middle of a stack of money to see if Hip-Hop would help them find the plug.

Forty-five minutes later, Uno saw the green dot stop at an address that popped onto the screen. Uno merged back into the lane and followed the directions. Uno pulled up in record time across the street from the address.

'What the fuck is he doing here?' Both Uno and LR wondered. Then it dawned on Uno what was happening.

"That's clever," Uno said.

A short, bold, cocky dude pulled up into the store parking lot in a Nissan truck. He hopped out, showing a gold chain with a medallion of a red dragon hanging below his belt. His diamond pinky ring glistened as he puffed on his blunt, surveyed the area, then said a few words in Hip-Hop's ear. He dropped the keys in his hand and walked into the back of the store. While surveying the area from the car, Uno was working his brain nonstop, trying to figure out where he knew the dude from.

Twenty minutes passed, and Hip-Hop was still gone. Uno and LR impatiently waited for Hip-Hop to return. Hip-Hop returned in the dude's car and parked in the same spot. He walked into the store, where he spent a few minutes. Hip-Hop cheerfully walked out of the store with a bag of Shea butter and hopped in his car. From the smile on his face, the deal went down without any problems.

Uno decided to make sure everything was everything, so he called Hip-Hop up.

"What it do, playboy?" Hip-Hop picked up and asked, speeding out of the parking lot.

"I was just checking in. We about a few hours away. Everything good ya way?" Uno asked.

"Everything is on the up. I'm headed ya way after I make these few moves," Hip-Hop replied.

Uno and LR sat in the car, watching Hip-Hop speed by them. "I'll holla at you when I get to the city," Uno said before he hung up.

They waited until they saw Hip-Hop's taillights disappearing down the road. Then, they slowly drove across the street and parked in the same spot Hip-Hop was in. They sat in the car for a few minutes so they could get their thoughts together.

Uno was contemplating whether he should take his gun or not because he didn't want to cause any trouble, but LR was thinking about all the cases they would be getting if this went through for them.

"Construct your own dreams," he said to LR before grabbing the briefcase out the backseat, and they walked into the store.

To their surprise, the store was packed.

"May I help you guys?" a beautiful, dark-skinned cashier asked. The cashier cheerfully smiled and nervously ran her fingers through her short hair while Uno admired her beauty.

LR slapped his arm, snapping him out of his daze.

"I'm sorry. It's just that when I see something as beautiful as yourself, cat gets my tongue," Uno charmed. "But I'm here for a meeting," he continued to talk.

"Okay, wait a minute." She smiled, then walked off.

As Uno walked through the store, the voice that was talking sounded so familiar. Uno scanned the store for the voice.

'I know I'm not tripping, but this setup looks like I been here before,' he said to himself as he stopped at the door of an office occupied by a group of men.

"I tell you what. That fuck boy Hip-Hop is so fucking soft! His mother must've thought he was supposed to be a female because he's all pussy!" Uno said.

The group started laughing, but quickly stopped when they noticed Uno standing in the doorway. The boss turned in his chair, and that was when he and Uno locked eyes with each other, trying to figure out where they knew each other from. The boss shut his eyes and had a quick flashback.

"Aye, my dude. You must be lost, standing there," one of the boss's men said, reaching for his gun before the boss stopped him.

"My bad. I'm here on business," Uno calmly said.

One of the men walked up to Uno and patted him down, and then he gave the boss a nod, letting him know he was clean.

The boss studied Uno from head to toe, shaking his head when he spotted the ring on his finger. "Wait a fucking minute! Where did that ring come from?" he asked Uno.

"I got it from my brother Big Dawg years ago. That's where," Uno blurted out proudly with his chest poked out.

"I knew you looked familiar. You must be Uno, the younger brother. I'm Jimmy," he said as he walked up to Uno and hugged him.

A huge smile appeared on Uno's face. He knew he knew that man from somewhere.

"Come and sit," Jimmy offered as he made everyone leave the office.

"Look at yourself. You're all grown up now! I haven't seen you since you were a little boy. Ever since Big Dawg and Ant stepped away from the streets, we haven't been connected," Jimmy said, smiling.

The beautiful cashier walked into the office and brought a bottle of wine to the table. She and Uno locked eyes for a minute before she disappeared.

"So, Uno, besides getting money, what have you been doing with yourself for these last few years?" Jimmy asked, pouring wine into their glasses.

"I just got out a while back from boys' school," Uno said, sipping his drink.

Jimmy then looked down and saw the briefcase sitting between Uno's legs and asked, "So what can I do for you?"

Uno sat back. "You know that nigga Hip-Hop who just left from here?"

Jimmy nodded his head, trying to figure out where Uno was going with bringing up Hip-Hop's name.

"Listen, Jimmy. I'm the nigga who's been spending," Uno said.

Jimmy leaned on his desk to hear more.

"Just like I effortlessly put a tracker in that duffel bag and followed him here to you today, what you think the Feds can do to him if they get their hands on him? He's a coward, and you know he's a liability to both of us. Neither one of us is trying to go to jail over a mindless dude," Uno said.

"So what is it that you bring to the table?" Jimmy gestured.

Uno grabbed the briefcase from between his legs, set it on the desk, and popped it open. Jimmy's eyes got as big as quarters when he saw what the contents were.

"There's three hundred thousand in here," Uno said, pushing the briefcase with a card containing his number to Jimmy. "I'm trying to cut out the middleman because I'm a boss," Uno said, standing up.

Jimmy studied Uno's face and saw something he saw in his own eyes when he was hugging the block—hunger and determination. He remembered seeing Uno when he was younger and predicted he was going to be something. Jimmy was a pretty good judge of character, and something in his stomach told him there was a bright future ahead for him and Uno.

"So, Uno, what type of price tag was you looking for?" Jimmy asked.

"I'm pretty sure you'll play fair for me. But keep in mind, the better my price tag is, the more competitive I'll be in the streets, which means cutting out the others, so the briefcase, like the one I just gave you, would double."

Jimmy twisted his pinky ring. "So, you're telling me here, right now, you can do three hundred thousand every weekend?"

Uno nodded his head. "At least! And if the price is right for me, then even more money," he said. "Listen, Jimmy. I have ambition, and me and my family are hungry. We tryna control the city. Yeah, I could have just went to my brothers and used their connections, but I'm my own man, so I'm here now with my own bread. I'm on something," Uno said, bending down to be eye level with Jimmy.

Jimmy sat back in his chair and chuckled. "I like your swag. I'm gonna do fifteen-five!"

"You have a deal!" Uno extended his hand for a shake.

Standing up, Jimmy patted Uno on his back. "Give me a few days to put things in order, and I'll give you a call," Jimmy said.

"I'll be ready," Uno said, headed for the door where he found LR talking to a female.

Uno walked out of the store with a newfound swag. He felt like his life was about to change.

Chapter 30

Two days later, Uno got a call. When he picked up the phone and heard Jimmy's voice, a lot of stress was lifted from his shoulders. Grabbing a pen and paper, he wrote down the address that was given to him, then thanked Jimmy and hung up with a smile. It was a house in Greenwood, and Jimmy's timing couldn't have been any better.

Uno called a meeting at Nasty's apartment. He drove like he was driving for the Indy 500. Uno smiled as he watched Tay-Tay ease out on the porch behind Nasty. She threw her arms around Nasty's neck and kissed his lips before Nasty walked down to the car and hopped in.

Uno just smiled, looking at him, before heading to their destination. The address Jimmy had given Uno was an address to a big ass house. Uno called the number he had and let whoever picked up know he was sitting in the driveway. They surveyed the area, waiting for someone to come out. The house had security cameras all over the place, right along with men armed with assault rifles walking around.

A short, fat dude dressed in slacks walked onto the porch and surveyed the area as he puffed on his cigar. The man motioned for Uno to pop his trunk. One of his men walked out with two big ass teddy bears, loaded them into the trunk, and then closed it.

Uno left the house and hopped straight on the highway, heading back to the city. He was in dire need of the vacation he and Punkin planned to go on the next day. The non-stop grinding was starting to take its toll on his body and mind.

The more money they made, the more problems there were to come, which he didn't mind, because every time money flowed in, it eased everything. He was already adding up their profits in his head. As they drove back, the car was quiet. All they were thinking about was getting back to the city and making all that money.

Nasty stared out the window and took in the beautiful view of Greenwood as they cruised the highway.

The two displayed smiles bigger than a fag with a bag of dicks in his hands when Uno pulled into the garage of the stash spot Mo-Mo was at.

Uno hit the keypad, making the garage shut. He popped open the trunk, grabbed the two bears containing the bricks, and headed inside. "Let's see what we got!" Uno said as he cut open one of the bears. A smile appeared on Uno's face as he pulled out each wrapped brick. He grabbed his pocketknife and went around the package to see what was there.

"That's that fish!" Mo-Mo said, looking at Uno and Nasty. "We finna get this paper!"

"Let's not celebrate too fast. We still have to see how it jumps back first," Uno responded as he headed into the kitchen with one of the bricks in his hand. Mo-Mo and Nasty were right on his heels.

Uno grabbed a pot from the cabinet, threw a little water in it, and set it on the stove until it started to boil. He weighed up one hundred grams while the pot heated up. He then dropped the dope and forty-six grams of baking soda into the pot when the water came to a boil. Nasty and Mo-Mo stared at Uno like he was a teacher in a classroom.

After putting in his work, Uno pulled the first batch from the pot. Instead of whipping, he straight dropped it to see what it jumped to. Both Mo-Mo and Nasty anxiously paced the floor as Uno walked over and set the cookie on the scale.

All three stared at each other in disbelief.

"It's a hundred and forty-six grams!" Uno smiled. "It's on now! They can't stop us!" Uno said.

"Now, it's time to bust this shit down!" Nasty said, ready to hit the streets.

Lock Down Publications and Ca$h Presents
Assisted Publishing Packages

Due to an increase in the price of services we have increased our prices. The prices below reflect the price increase as of 11/1/24.

BASIC PACKAGE $699 Editing Cover Design Formatting	UPGRADED PACKAGE $1000 Typing Editing Cover Design Formatting Upload eBooks to Amazon Upload Paperback to Amazon
ADVANCE PACKAGE $1,400 Typing Editing (line editing/content) Cover Design Formatting Copyright Registration Proofreading Upload eBooks to Amazon Upload Paperback to Amazon	LDP SUPREME PACKAGE $1,700 Typing Editing (line editing/content) Cover Design Formatting Copyright Registration Proofreading Set up Amazon Account Upload eBooks to Amazon Upload Paperback to Amazon Advertise on LDP's Amazon and Facebook Page

***

Other services available upon request.
Additional charges may apply

Lock Down Publications
P.O. Box 944
Stockbridge, GA 30281-9998
Phone: 470 303-9761
Email: lockdownpublications@gmail.com

Submission Guideline

Submit the first three chapters of your completed manuscript to ldpsubmissions@gmail.com. In the subject line add **Your Book's Title**. The manuscript must be in a Word Doc file and sent as an attachment. Document should be in Times New Roman, double spaced, and in size 12 font. Also, provide your synopsis and full contact information. If sending multiple submissions, they must each be in a separate email.

Have a story but no way to send it electronically? You can still submit to LDP/Ca$h Presents. Send in the first three chapters, written or typed, of your completed manuscript to:

LDP: Submissions Dept
P.O. Box 944
Stockbridge, GA 30281-9998

DO NOT send original manuscript. Must be a duplicate. Provide your synopsis and a cover letter containing your full contact information.

Thanks for considering LDP and Ca$h Presents.

NEW RELEASES

BLOODLINE OF A SAVAGE 1-3
THESE VICIOUS STREETS 1-3
RELENTLESS GOON 1-3
BY PRINCE A. TAUHID

THE BUTTERFLY MAFIA 1-3
BY FUMIYA PAYNE

A THUG'S STREET PRINCESS 1&2
BY MEESHA

CITY OF SMOKE 3
BY MOLOTTI

GET IT IN SLUGS 1 &2
BY B. STALL

STANDING ON HER BUSINESS 1&2
BY DG SANTANA

STEPPERS 1,2&3
THE REAL BADDIES OF CHI-RAQ
BY KING RIO

THE LANE 1&2
BY KEN-KEN SPENCE

THUG OF SPADES 1&2
LOVE IN THE TRENCHES 2
CORNER BOYS
BY COREY ROBINSON

TIL DEATH 3
BY ARYANNA

THE BIRTH OF A GANGSTER 4
BY DELMONT PLAYER

PRODUCT OF THE STREETS 1-3
BY DEMOND "MONEY" ANDERSON

NO TIME FOR ERROR
BY KEESE

MONEY HUNGRY DEMONS 1-2
BY TRANAY ADAMS

HUB CITY MENACE 1-3
BY J. WHITE

A THUGGISH PASSION 1&2
LAND OF DA HOOLIGANZ 1-4
KILLAZ ON STANDBY 1&2
BY IRA B.

FO'EVA ROLLIN 1&2
BY ASSA RAYMOND BAKER

THE LEVEL UP 1&3
BY LUXURY KING

Coming Soon from Lock Down Publications/Ca$h Presents

IF YOU CROSS ME ONCE 6
ANGEL V
By Anthony Fields

A THUGS STREET PRINCESS 3
By Meesha

CORNER BOYS 2
By Corey Robinson

THA TAKEOVER
By Keith Chandler

BETRAYAL OF A G 2
By Ray Vinci

SAVAGE FAMILY EMPIRE 1&2
SOULLESS GOON 1,2&3
THE DIRTY SIDE OF MONEY 1,2&3
By Prince

FOR MY ENEMY'S SAKE
AMBITIONS OF A SLIDER
FRESH OFF DA PORCH
By IRA B.

THE TRUCKLOAD 1-4
TIPPIN' THE SCALES 1-3
BAD BITCHES WIT GUNZ 3
PROBLEM SOLVED 2
By Christopher "Diesel" Hornezes

Available Now

RESTRAINING ORDER 1 & 2
By **CA$H & Coffee**

LOVE KNOWS NO BOUNDARIES 1-3
By **Coffee**

RAISED AS A GOON I, II, III & IV
BRED BY THE SLUMS I, II, III
BLAST FOR ME I & II
ROTTEN TO THE CORE I II III
A BRONX TALE I, II, III
DUFFLE BAG CARTEL I II III IV V VI
HEARTLESS GOON I II III IV V
A SAVAGE DOPEBOY I II
DRUG LORDS I II III
CUTTHROAT MAFIA I II
KING OF THE TRENCHES
By **Ghost**

LAY IT DOWN I & II
LAST OF A DYING BREED I II
BLOOD STAINS OF A SHOTTA I & II III
By **Jamaica**

LOYAL TO THE GAME I II III
LIFE OF SIN I, II III
By **TJ & Jelissa**

IF LOVING HIM IS WRONG…I & II
LOVE ME EVEN WHEN IT HURTS I II III
By **Jelissa**

PUSH IT TO THE LIMIT
By **Bre' Hayes**

BLOODY COMMAS I & II
SKI MASK CARTEL I, II & III
KING OF NEW YORK I II, III IV V
RISE TO POWER I II III
COKE KINGS I II III IV V
BORN HEARTLESS I II III IV
KING OF THE TRAP I II
By **T.J. Edwards**

WHEN THE STREETS CLAP BACK I & II III
THE HEART OF A SAVAGE I II III IV
MONEY MAFIA I II
LOYAL TO THE SOIL I II III
By **Jibril Williams**

A DISTINGUISHED THUG STOLE MY HEART I II & III
LOVE SHOULDN'T HURT I II III IV
RENEGADE BOYS 1-4
PAID IN KARMA 1-3
SAVAGE STORMS 1-3
AN UNFORESEEN LOVE 1-3
BABY, I'M WINTERTIME COLD 1-3
A THUG'S STREET PRINCESS 1&2
By **Meesha**

A GANGSTER'S CODE 1-3
A GANGSTER'S SYN 1-3
THE SAVAGE LIFE 1-3
CHAINED TO THE STREETS 1-3
BLOOD ON THE MONEY 1-3
A GANGSTA'S PAIN 1-3
BEAUTIFUL LIES AND UGLY TRUTHS
CHURCH IN THESE STREETS
By **J-Blunt**

CUM FOR ME 1-8
An LDP Erotica Collaboration

BLOOD OF A BOSS 1-5
SHADOWS OF THE GAME
TRAP BASTARD
By **Askari**

THE STREETS BLEED MURDER 1-3
THE HEART OF A GANGSTA 1-3
By **Jerry Jackson**

WHEN A GOOD GIRL GOES BAD
By **Adrienne**

THE COST OF LOYALTY 1-3
By **Kweli**

BRIDE OF A HUSTLA 1-3
THE FETTI GIRLS 1-3
CORRUPTED BY A GANGSTA 1-4
BLINDED BY HIS LOVE
THE PRICE YOU PAY FOR LOVE 1-3
DOPE GIRL MAGIC 1-3
By **Destiny Skai**

A KINGPIN'S AMBITION
A KINGPIN'S AMBITION II
I MURDER FOR THE DOUGH
By **Ambitious**

TRUE SAVAGE 1-7
DOPE BOY MAGIC 1-3
MIDNIGHT CARTEL 1-3
CITY OF KINGZ 1&2
NIGHTMARE ON SILENT AVE
THE PLUG OF LIL MEXICO 1&2
CLASSIC CITY
By **Chris Green**

A GANGSTER'S REVENGE 1-4
THE BOSS MAN'S DAUGHTERS 1-5
A SAVAGE LOVE 1&2
BAE BELONGS TO ME 1&2
A HUSTLER'S DECEIT 1-3
WHAT BAD BITCHES DO 1-3
SOUL OF A MONSTER 1-3
KILL ZONE
A DOPE BOY'S QUEEN 1-3
TIL DEATH 1-3
IMMA DIE BOUT MINE 1-6
DYING FOR LIKES
By **Aryanna**

A DOPEBOY'S PRAYER
By **Eddie "Wolf" Lee**

THE KING CARTEL 1-3
By **Frank Gresham**

THESE NIGGAS AIN'T LOYAL 1-3
By **Nikki Tee**

GANGSTA SHYT 1-3
By **CATO**

THE ULTIMATE BETRAYAL
By **Phoenix**

BOSS'N UP 1-3
By **Royal Nicole**

I LOVE YOU TO DEATH
By **Destiny J**

I RIDE FOR MY HITTA
I STILL RIDE FOR MY HITTA
By **Misty Holt**

LOVE & CHASIN' PAPER
By **Qay Crockett**

TO DIE IN VAIN
SINS OF A HUSTLA
By **ASAD**

BROOKLYN HUSTLAZ
By **Boogsy Morina**

BROOKLYN ON LOCK 1 & 2
By **Sonovia**

GANGSTA CITY
By **Teddy Duke**

A DRUG KING AND HIS DIAMOND 1-3
A DOPEMAN'S RICHES
HER MAN, MINE'S TOO 1&2
CASH MONEY HO'S
THE WIFEY I USED TO BE 1&2
PRETTY GIRLS DO NASTY THINGS
By **Nicole Goosby**

LIPSTICK KILLAH 1-3
CRIME OF PASSION 1-3
FRIEND OR FOE 1-3
By **Mimi**

TRAPHOUSE KING 1-3
KINGPIN KILLAZ 1-3
STREET KINGS 1&2
PAID IN BLOOD 1&2
CARTEL KILLAZ 1-3
DOPE GODS 1&2
By **Hood Rich**

THE STREETS ARE CALLING
By **Duquie Wilson**

STEADY MOBBN' 1-3
THE STREETS STAINED MY SOUL 1-3
By **Marcellus Allen**

WHO SHOT YA 1-3
SON OF A DOPE FIEND 1-4
HEAVEN GOT A GHETTO 1&2
SKI MASK MONEY 1&2
By **Renta**

GORILLAZ IN THE BAY 1-4
TEARS OF A GANGSTA 1/&2
3X KRAZY 1&2
STRAIGHT BEAST MODE 1&2
By **DE'KARI**

TRIGGADALE 1-3
MURDA WAS THE CASE 1-3
By **Elijah R. Freeman**

SLAUGHTER GANG 1-3
RUTHLESS HEART 1-3
By **Willie Slaughter**

GOD BLESS THE TRAPPERS 1-3
THESE SCANDALOUS STREETS 1-3
FEAR MY GANGSTA 1-5
THESE STREETS DON'T LOVE NOBODY 1-2
BURY ME A G 1-5
A GANGSTA'S EMPIRE 1-4
THE DOPEMAN'S BODYGAURD 1&2
THE REALEST KILLAZ 1-3
THE LAST OF THE OGS 1-3
By **Tranay Adams**

MARRIED TO A BOSS 1-3
By **Destiny Skai & Chris Green**

KINGZ OF THE GAME 1-7
CRIME BOSS 1-4
By **Playa Ray**

FUK SHYT
By **Blakk Diamond**

DON'T F#CK WITH MY HEART 1&2
By **Linnea**

ADDICTED TO THE DRAMA 1-3
IN THE ARM OF HIS BOSS
By **Jamila**

LOYALTY AIN'T PROMISED 1&2
By **Keith Williams**

YAYO 1-4
A SHOOTER'S AMBITION 1&2
BRED IN THE GAME
By **S. Allen**

TRAP GOD 1-3
RICH $AVAGE 1-3
MONEY IN THE GRAVE 1-3
CARTEL MONEY 1&2
By **Martell Troublesome Bolden**

FOREVER GANGSTA 1&2
GLOCKS ON SATIN SHEETS 1&2
By **Adrian Dulan**

TOE TAGZ 1-4
LEVELS TO THIS SHYT 1&2
IT'S JUST ME AND YOU
By **Ah'Million**

KINGPIN DREAMS 1-3
RAN OFF ON DA PLUG
By **Paper Boi Rari**

THE STREETS MADE ME 1-3
By **Larry D. Wright**

CONFESSIONS OF A GANGSTA 1-4
CONFESSIONS OF A JACKBOY 1-3
CONFESSIONS OF A HITMAN
CONFESSIONS OF A DOPE BOY
By **Nicholas Lock**

I'M NOTHING WITHOUT HIS LOVE
SINS OF A THUG
TO THE THUG I LOVED BEFORE
A GANGSTA SAVED XMAS
IN A HUSTLER I TRUST
By **Monet Dragun**

QUIET MONEY 1-3
THUG LIFE 1-3
EXTENDED CLIP 1&2
A GANGSTA'S PARADISE
By **Trai'Quan**

CAUGHT UP IN THE LIFE 1-3
THE STREETS NEVER LET GO 1-3
By **Robert Baptiste**

NEW TO THE GAME 1-3
MONEY, MURDER & MEMORIES 1-3
By **Malik D. Rice**

CREAM 2-3
THE STREETS WILL TALK
By **Yolanda Moore**

THE STREETS WILL NEVER CLOSE 1-3
By **K'ajji**

LIFE OF A SAVAGE 1-4
A GANGSTA'S QUR'AN 1-4
MURDA SEASON 1-3
GANGLAND CARTEL 1-3
CHI'RAQ GANGSTAS 1-4
KILLERS ON ELM STREET 1-3
JACK BOYZ N DA BRONX 1-3
A DOPEBOY'S DREAM 1-3
JACK BOYS VS DOPE BOYS 1-3
COKE GIRLZ
COKE BOYS
SOSA GANG 1&2
BRONX SAVAGES
BODYMORE KINGPINS
BLOOD OF A GOON
By **Romell Tukes**

CONCRETE KILLA 1-3
VICIOUS LOYALTY 1-3
BLOODY MONEY BAGS
By **Kingpen**

THE ULTIMATE SACRIFICE 1-6
KHADIFI
IF YOU CROSS ME ONCE 1-3
ANGEL 1-4
IN THE BLINK OF AN EYE
By **Anthony Fields**

THE LIFE OF A HOOD STAR
By **Ca$h & Rashia Wilson**

NIGHTMARES OF A HUSTLA 1-3
BLOOD AND GAMES 1&2
By **King Dream**

GHOST MOB
By **Stilloan Robinson**

HARD AND RUTHLESS 1&2
MOB TOWN 251
THE BILLIONAIRE BENTLEYS 1-3
REAL G'S MOVE IN SILENCE
By **Von Diesel**

MOB TIES 1-7
SOUL OF A HUSTLER, HEART OF A KILLER 1-3
GORILLAZ IN THE TRENCHES
OOPS CRY TOO 1&2
THE DAUGHTER OF A CARTEL BOSS
By **SayNoMore**

BODYMORE MURDERLAND 1-3
THE BIRTH OF A GANGSTER 1-4
By **Delmont Player**

FOR THE LOVE OF A BOSS 1&2
By **C. D. Blue**

KILLA KOUNTY 1-5
TENDER
By **Khufu**

MOBBED UP 1-4
THE BRICK MAN 1-5
THE COCAINE PRINCESS 1-10
STEPPERS 1-3
SUPER GREMLIN 1-4
A GANGSTA'S SON
By **King Rio**

MONEY GAME 1&2
By **Smoove Dolla**

A GANGSTA'S KARMA 1-5
By **FLAME**

KING OF THE TRENCHES 1-3
By **GHOST & TRANAY ADAMS**

BAD BITCHES WIT GUNZ 1&2
PROBLEM SOLVED
By **"Christopher Diesel" Hornezes**

QUEEN OF THE ZOO 1&2
By **Black Migo**

GRIMEY WAYS 1-3
BETRAYAL OF A G
By **Ray Vinci**

XMAS WITH AN ATL SHOOTER
By **Ca$h & Destiny Skai**

KING KILLA 1&2
By **Vincent "Vitto" Holloway**

BETRAYAL OF A THUG 1&2
By **Fre$h**

COUNTDOWN OF A KILLA 1&2
SEX, MURDER AND GOD 1&2
GUNS DOWN, BOTTOMS UP 1&2
By **Lo-Life**

THE MURDER QUEENS 1-7
By **Michael Gallon**

FOR THE LOVE OF BLOOD 1-4
By **Jamel Mitchell**

THA TAKEOVER 2 | KEITH CHANDLER

HOOD CONSIGLIERE 1&2
NO TIME FOR ERROR
By **Keese**

PROTÉGÉ OF A LEGEND 1,2&3
LOVE IN THE TRENCHES 1&2
By **Corey Robinson**

THE PLUG'S RUTHLESS DAUGHTER 1&2
By **Tony Daniels**

BORN IN THE GRAVE 1-3
CRIME PAYS
By **Self Made Tay**

MOAN IN MY MOUTH
By **XTASY**

TORN BETWEEN A GANGSTER AND A GENTLEMAN
By **J-BLUNT & Miss Kim**

LOYALTY IS EVERYTHING 1-3
CITY OF SMOKE 1-3
By **Molotti**

HERE TODAY GONE TOMORROW 1&2
By **Fly Rock**

WOMEN LIE MEN LIE 1-4
FIFTY SHADES OF SNOW 1-3
STACK BEFORE YOU SPLURGE
GIRLS FALL LIKE DOMINOES
NAÏVE TO THE STREETS
By **ROY MILLIGAN**

PILLOW PRINCESS
By **S. Hawkins**

THE BUTTERFLY MAFIA 1-3
SALUTE MY SAVAGERY 1&2
By **Fumiya Payne**

THE LANE 1&2
By Ken-Ken Spence

THE PUSSY TRAP 1-5
By **Nene Capri**

DIRTY DNA
By **Blaque**

SANCTIFIED AND HORNY
by **XTASY**

BOOKS BY LDP'S CEO, CA$H

TRUST IN NO MAN
TRUST IN NO MAN 2
TRUST IN NO MAN 3
BONDED BY BLOOD
SHORTY GOT A THUG
THUGS CRY
THUGS CRY 2
THUGS CRY 3
TRUST NO BITCH
TRUST NO BITCH 2
TRUST NO BITCH 3
TIL MY CASKET DROPS
RESTRAINING ORDER
RESTRAINING ORDER 2
IN LOVE WITH A CONVICT
LIFE OF A HOOD STAR
XMAS WITH AN ATL SHOOTER

www.ingramcontent.com/pod-product-compliance
Lightning Source LLC
Chambersburg PA
CBHW070520260626
47161CB00004B/1594